Visions ot Gaea

Ascension

Story by

R. R. Vaz

Table of Contents

Darm in the year 99 of the Age of Enlightenment

    Prologue

Part I – A long-expected Gathering

    First memory – Accounts of a remote past

    Second memory - Nightfall in the White Metropolis

    Third memory – When drifters race

    Fourth memory – At the East Retreat

    Fifth memory – Anatomy of a virus

    Sixth memory – Tales of the long departed

    Seventh memory – The Database

    Eighth memory – Desperate Measures

    Ninth memory – Of young and old ancestors

    Tenth memory – The Gathering

    Eleventh memory – Fugitives in Darm

Prelude to Ascension

Glossary

Story by: R.R.Vaz
Cover by: Andreas Rocha
Translated to English by: R.R.Vaz
English revision by: Asha Self
Last update: 11-12-19
ISBN: 978-167-44291-7-5

© 2012 R.R.Vaz. All rights reserved. The following content may not be modified in any form, or by any means reproduced or distributed without permission of the author. Visions of Gaea is under the protection of the Berne Convention and the DMCA; any attempt of plagiarism or piracy may be prosecuted in accordance with international laws. Please support artists by buying original art on official retailers.

Foreword: Visions of Gaea employs second-person narrative. Readers are asked to understand that this is not the author's attempt at experimenting with narrative modes, but rather comes as a direct consequence of the storyline.
In addition, these visions have a strong speculative component regarding future technologies. To ensure an optimal reading experience the glossary provides a summarized description of each of them, while a more extensive description and bonus content is available at www.visionsofgaia.com.

Darm in the year 99 of the Age of Enlightenment

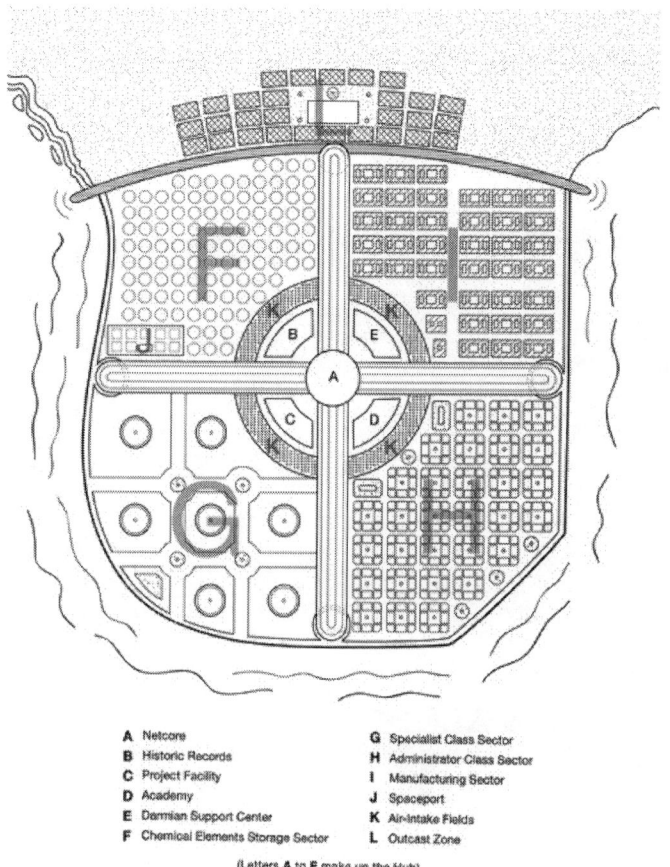

A Netcore
B Historic Records
C Project Facility
D Academy
E Darmian Support Center
F Chemical Elements Storage Sector
G Specialist Class Sector
H Administrator Class Sector
I Manufacturing Sector
J Spaceport
K Air-Intake Fields
L Outcast Zone

(Letters A to E make up the Hub)

For you,

Lost men from the past, hear me out,
for what is to be told must not be forgotten.
These events have not yet come to pass,
yet I have known them since The Beginning.
When your kind ceased to exist, your great deeds faded from memory
and from the ruins of your once proud cities
a new kind arose...the Pyre.
This is when this story begins.
It is story about love,
in a time when its meaning had been lost.
It is a story of adventure,
in a frozen world known as Artica.
Above all, it is also the tale of Alan Balthazar,
the last of your kind.
Know his name.
Learn his fate.
For that which has been forgotten must be remembered,
if you are to survive The End that is upon you...

Prologue

A dark figure cloaked in a hooded cape trudged along a muddy path in a dense misty forest. Its sluggish gait resembled that of a sleepwalker stepping noisily on shallow puddles and tangled roots, following the pale green glow of fruits that hung from the thick canopy. A mournful cry wailed through the mist, and in a slow vigilant gaze the cold, grim countenance of a pyrean was revealed from beneath the lowered hood. His name is of no importance, for there was no one to utter it in that forgotten forest, which apart from the faint droning of the glowing fruits seemed immersed in a deep slumber. Her memories seemed stored in the stagnant fragrance of Her flowers, and the mottled bark from Her tall broad trunks seemed to depict tales as primeval as the dawn of life. There was no one to utter it, but Her.

Carelessly trampling the undergrowth that had claimed the path, doubt began to reawaken him, forcing him to reconsider his decision in entering Her domain, compelling him to believe that She had deceived him in a final gesture of punishment. Wrapped in that treacherous doubt, it took him some time to realize the ever increasing glow of the fruits, which now provided him with a clearer sight of the path ahead. As he trod onward, the undergrowth became greener, the flowers livelier, and the crooked roots sprung stronger from the colossal trunks which had become twice as large and countless times taller than him. The mist slowly dispersed and he was granted the distant vision of a glade laying bare to the silvery night. Confidence warmed his blood and banished all his doubts, for he knew he was arriving at the heart of the forest, the cradle of Nature, Her dwelling.

As he approached the glade, his black boots enveloped in the dormant mist, he took his first step on solid ground, and as he looked down he saw the path had turned into worn stepping stones that ended further ahead, at the porch of a small wooden cottage standing at the centre of the glade. It seemed abandoned, reclaimed by Nature, with thick moss covering the deformed roof and fungi sprouting from the darkened walls.

He approached it, resolute.

A rocking chair swung eerily on the porch, fanned by an unfelt breeze. His heavy footsteps on the wooden floor creaked from the porch to the glade and from the glade to the forest, rendering the chair to a still silence. He approached the door, and when his dark glove was about to touch the rusty handle, something stopped him: a fleeting whisper floating with the breeze summoned him to the back of the cottage. She was calling to him, so he answered without hesitation.

And so it was that after countless days of wandering he found Her, sitting quietly on a stone bench in front of a moss laden well. A hood draped over Her face and She was huddled in a worn gray mantle that hid Her body. At her waist, a thick rope tied the mantle to Her withered form.

'At last I find you, witch,' he muttered in an accursed tone as he stopped before Her.

She seemed oblivious to his presence, rather focused on splitting leaves from a crooked branch and placing them in a pestle resting next to Her on the stone bench.

'That is no manner to address the one who spared you from death,' She uttered inattentively, Her haunting voice but a fleeting breeze.

When she picked the last leaf, the branch faded from Her hand, turning into mist that scattered through the heavy air. She placed the leaf on the pestle and pulled back Her hood, revealing Herself to him.

She donned the appearance of an elder lady, but Her wrinkled face lacked skin, flesh or bone, and Her long translucent hair was as silvery as the rays of light that shone upon Her head. She seemed older than the forest, older than time itself even, and Her ethereal shape betrayed Her as a divine entity whose lingering on the material plane had withered her grace.

'Death,' he muttered, impressed by Her appearance. 'For so long I have felt without life yet the meaning of that word still eludes me.'

She gave him a kind smile. 'And yet, here you are, searching for the meaning of both,' she uttered, her voice a pleased breeze. 'Tell me, when was the last time you shed a tear?'

His shadowed eyes glinted with displeasure from underneath the hood for he knew just what She intended to ask. It had been so long since last they met, yet still She clung to the hope that he could be rescued from the emptiness that had consumed him.

After a fleeting silence he raised his head proudly. 'I bear the burden of tears no more, witch,' he said. 'They have dried out, along with my past.'

Upon hearing him, Her smile faded and She turned once again to Her task. With Her ethereal hands She picked up the pestle and mortar and started crushing the stack of leaves and petals inside it. When they began forming a thick blue paste, their fragrance was released to the dormant glade. It was a soft and soothing scent, and wherever it spread, the saturated air became as fresh as a spring breeze.

'This forest is ancient,' she uttered. 'It holds a power that no living creature can tame.'

As he thoughtlessly inhaled the air, he sensed a change in him. The burden of carrying his body had lightened, and his mind was visited by visions of long forgotten places. Surrendering himself to the growing tranquillity, he raised his head to the silvery night and his hood fell on his back, laying bare a cold deathly face and long black hair. He closed his eyes and took a deep breath, filling his mind with the soothing fragrance. His chest grew beyond the black cape and as the fine thread holding it around his neck untied, the cape fell to the ground, revealing all at once his grand shape. He was strong and menacing, and wore a plain crimson tunic tucked under a dark belt adorned with intricate patterns of gold. On his robust legs he wore a pair of black breeches tucked into the tall boots.

'What a pyrean you have become,' remarked the ethereal figure, whose meagre size was half his stature. 'The first I met you, you were but a scrawny boy. Now you have become great beyond comparison.'

'Pyrean?' he asked bitterly, opening his eyes. 'No. There is no Pyre left in me.'

She seemed under the influence of a powerful spell. Her shape, once elder and ethereal, had become the youthful and gracious embodiment of Nature. Her gray cloak had dissolved into weightless red leaves that floated freely about Her bare body. Her skin had become tree bark and Her hair green strands of vine, and the delicate features of Her cinnamon face were of an unmatched beauty, paling in comparison only to the irresistible calling of Her deep green eyes. She rose from the stone bench and placed a palm on his chest, the touch flooding his body with a renewed calmness.

'Do not lose faith. That boy lives on inside you. You lost sight of him only because you stopped looking,' she uttered, and her haunting voice carried an alluring kindness. 'No one ever truly dies. There is a part of us that is eternal. And that part, whether you want it or not, not even death can erase.'

The pyrean lowered his eyes, humbled by Her unbridled grace, 'It is only by your will that I still live.' He raised his head proudly and spoke, 'I have answered Your calling. Tell me what You will have me do or release me from my vow for I do not wish to linger here any longer.'

'I will have you do nothing,' She said firmly, 'but to look into the Well of Souls. It is there that your oath shall be redeemed, and the answers that you seek found. It is there that you will know your true self, in the memories of the past.'

He gazed at her intense green eyes and spoke with resolve, 'If that is all You ask of me, so be it.'

She turned to grab the mortar containing the finished mixture and walked to a cauldron boiling on a fire at the back of the wooden cottage. She dripped the liquefied paste into the bubbling water and stirred it with a long wooden spoon, whispering an indecipherable chant. After it had coagulated into a glowing blue soup she picked up a nearby silver ewer and dipped it in the cauldron. Bearing the ewer in Her hands, She walked back to the well, the weightless flowers floating around Her body leaving a trail behind.

As the pyrean walked to Her side, She uttered in a tranquil voice, 'Certain pasts are too terrible to be remembered. Others are too important to be forgotten. Yours lies in the middle: a tragic past that fate has decided to remember, perhaps because it may lead to a brighter future.'

Despite being deeply enthralled, his voice was steady, 'There is no past more terrible than an empty present.'

She took one sip from the ewer and then offered it to him.

'I give you the Essence of Life. Taste of it so that we may begin our crossing. It is a journey we shall take together through the untameable Tides of Fate. I shall be your guide and I shall do all within my power to help you remember.'

The pyrean accepted it, snatching it with a brute hand. Then he drank without hesitation one mouthful of the warm soup. Its taste was intense and difficult to withstand, and while it lingered in his mouth he saw every event that had come before his time with unparalleled clarity. He saw the birth of the Cosmos, of its stars and galaxies, of star systems and planets and moons, and the birth of Life itself. He swallowed the essence, for he was unable to bear the ever growing and overwhelming depth of the visions any further.

With a trembling hand he returned the ewer. She poured the remainder in the dark stale water of the well and invited him to look upon it.

As he stooped over the edge, he saw the glowing blue soup sink into an inscrutable depth and disappear. For a moment, there was a stony silence in the glade. Then, the earth began rumbling at his feet and the trees rustling in a growing wind, as an intense speck of light emerged in the depths of the well. The water stirred and stirred and grew into a whirlpool, and as the earth trembled wildly and the trees rustled restlessly, the speck of light came surging to the surface, its brightness kindling the glade. Then, as unexpectedly as it had begun, the water calmed down, the earth rested, and the trees fell asleep.

When he looked once more into the water, he saw its surface had become as calm and scintillating as the clearest mirror he had ever laid eyes upon. It reflected his undaunted gaze with a foreboding stillness. As he looked at the strange mirror, waiting to see an image of his past, he was overtaken by a strange weakness that quickly overpowered him and sent his knees to the ground. He grabbed the edge of the well as his face was pulled towards his reflection with an inexorable force. His eyes stared at him from the reflection with astonished surprise and as he stared back an unbreakable bond ensnared him in an undeniable contemplation.

A prophetic voice carried from far beyond arrived at his ears, 'Through the Well of Souls you shall see the course of events. Memories of moments passed, of countless lives whose bodies have turned to dust. Stories that were left untold shall unravel themselves clearer than any remembrance. You shall see who you were, and when you return, you will know who you are.

'Tempus praeteritum videre.'

Time stood still that instant. His body remained frozen, looming over the well. His consciousness was gently separated from his body and carried away to a distant quiet place. He felt far from himself, detached, alone, and he closed his eyes. When he reopened them, he was immersed in an empty brightness, an eternal white in perfect harmony with the distant chanting of an unseen choir. It was all so calm, so tranquil and at peace. He felt free, and so he marvelled at the melody and basked in the warmth that embraced him. The boundless white was gradually filled with never-ending specks of colours, and as they floated through him he heard indistinct voices, children's laughter. He had time to draw a smile before all white and colours, all voices and laughter converged abruptly in front of him into one light, one note, one single breath of time that ended in an immensurable collapse that delivered him to a complete and silent darkness.

A pure soothing voice broke the silence:

'Awake now from your eternal slumber and relive your past.'

'Awake!' said a voice, now in a demanding tone.

Part I – A long-expected Gathering

First memory – Accounts of a remote past

'Wake up apprentice Alan!' yelled mentor Levine.

You flinched on your chair and opened your eyes. The feeling that you were in trouble quickly roused you to a state of full awareness. Glancing from one side to the other, you found her straight ahead, sitting behind her desk above the dais. Eyes locked on her sharp stare, you sat up straight and calmly placed your hands on your desk.

'Given that you are such an expert on this topic that you need not stay awake, you shall clarify for us the first details pertaining to the beginning of the Age of Obscurity,' she said.

From the silence that followed you could hear the whisperings of some of your fellow apprentices complaining about the interruption.

The mentor placed her forearms on the plain metal desk, clasped her hands and beckoned firmly, 'Apprentice Balthazar, time does not stand still,' she said, this time employing your surname as was formally required.

...Alan Balthazar...that was my name...

You looked at her with defiance, and above the whisperings you calmly asked, 'The official account or the truth?'

The indoctrination room was instantly immersed in a dumbfounded silence as every apprentice straightened in their chairs and looked directly ahead.

The mentor rose from her seat, staring at you gravely. 'Be very cautious in choosing your next words apprentice Balthazar, for if they are not what I expect to hear I shall personally escort you to a group of Overseers.'

You hid your uneasiness under a calm expression, knowing you had gone too far. You would not dare disobey her, for you had experience of how disturbing a session with Council Overseers could be: strenuous hours of interrogation, followed by a long wait for the results, but worst of all, their subversive speech which seemed more like a subliminal way of compelling you to obedience rather than a simple reprimand.

'My apology, mentor Levine,' you answered, a sober look on your face. 'It was not my intention to show disrespect.'

The mentor did not react immediately. During the uncomfortable silence that followed she merely gave you a dull stare.

'Apology accepted, apprentice Balthazar,' she suddenly mumbled with indifference.

Slowly and wearily, she sat back on her chair and resumed the indoctrination as though nothing had happened, continuing to address the circumstances that led to the extinction of the Antiga Pyre:

'With the analysis of recently discovered artifacts it has become clear to us that the collapse of antigan civilization is directly related to the emergence of the retrovirus PIn-T2. Although in some cases it would not terminate the existence of its host, this retrovirus was incurable and highly contagious. As such, it rapidly spread throughout antigan societies and destroyed them from within, either by infecting their inhabitants or by forcing them to flee,' she said and stopped to take a sip of water from the cup on top of the desk only to continue at the monotonous pace of her ever parching lips. 'Archaeological evidence further suggests that the end of antigan civilization was marked by the antigan's last effort to contain the pandemic with the construction of self-sustained safe-havens. Despite ensuring the safety of their residents, these save-havens proved to be unsuccessful in stopping the invasion of infected pyreans without terminating their existence, and in the centuries of genocide that followed, the Antiga Pyre slipped to the brink of self-extinction.'

As you waited for the end of the indoctrination you struggled to focus your attention on her less than plump face and short gray hair, yet from time to time you could not resist looking outside the window-wall behind her. The sky was a pale shade of orange, the sign that Mithras was setting and the indoctrination was soon coming to an end. You were anxious for that moment, for you and Haji had planned to spend the rest of the afternoon at the Shelter.

Haji, however, was paying due attention, sitting at the desk next to yours and listening to every word the mentor spoke. When she busied herself for a moment to prepare the next holographic projection, he gave you a sympathetic smile to demonstrate his solidarity. Instead of feeling sorry for yourself, you threw him a wicked grin.

Suddenly, a three-dimensional projection of Artica highlighting the last pockets of antigan civilization was displayed above the *holoprojector*[1] placed on the centre of the days.

'There are few recovered artifacts of the subsequent Age of Obscurity,' mentor Levine continued, 'nevertheless, these allowed us to determine that the save-havens were ultimately overtaken and their inhabitants infected, and during the following millennia the remaining antigans spread throughout Artica, some adopting a nomadic form of existence, others constructing small crude encampments that were presumably unable to grow beyond haphazard settlements. It was during these six thousand years of obscurity that the legacy of the antigan civilization was lost and the genetic mutation caused by the retrovirus settled into the gene pool of the Pyre as it was carried on from generation to generation, unchecked, unhindered. Ultimately, this mutation led the last survivors of the Antiga Pyre to evolve into a new species, we, the Nova Pyre,' mentor Levine stated, her dull voice hindering your task of answering the feedback questions that were being continuously sent to your *neuropad*[2].

'The Age of Obscurity was a time of ignorance and savagery, but it was during that time, and in such inhospitable conditions, that a pyrean rose up and rescued the Pyre from slow but inevitable extinction. After decades of isolation on the most ancient and reclusive laboratory of the Nova Pyre, Gadim conceived a device capable of suppressing our genetic flaw, thus putting an end to the Age of Obscurity and giving rise the Age of Enlightenment. It was then that Gadim came to be our illustrious Guiding Father. It was then, that in His great wisdom, He created the Personal Identification Unit,' she said and became quiet, casting her drooping eyes upon each of the apprentices.

A murmur spread throughout the room as some apprentices muttered amongst themselves, some pointing, others staring at their left forearms. Because she was pleased with their suspicion, mentor Levine expressed her only smile throughout the entire year. It was but a thin bent line on her lips, yet given it was coming from her, it was as big of a display of joy as laughing.

'Precisely,' she resumed with a withered enthusiasm, 'the inconspicuous membrane bound to your left forearm is far more extraordinary than it appears to be. Despite its simplicity, it represents the ingenuity of the Pyre in overcoming the retrovirus that put an end to our ancestors and is one of the two core technologies that ensure the functionality of our prototype metropolis. The Unit, as it is commonly referred to, is not only capable of regulating and monitoring our vital functions but also of blocking the genetic flaw caused by the retrovirus,' pausing for a moment to recover her breath, she drank the last sip of water from the cup and resumed. 'The second core technology of Darm and the second most important achievement of our Guiding Father, is the artificial intelligence that safeguards the order in our metropolis. She resides in the Netcore and readily performs the invaluable and interminable task of monitoring and processing all the activities performed by every citizen and apprentice in Darm, an exemplary performance which has awarded her the title of Mother. In sum, it is only because of these two technologies that the Nova Pyre was allowed to build a sustainable and prosperous metropolis, without ignorance or savagery, without quarrel or idleness, and most important of all, free from the affliction that affected the Pyre since the dawn of the Age of Obscurity. It is a brilliant accomplishment, one that has allowed us to uphold the order in our society,' she said, her eyes jumping from apprentice to apprentice and finally resting on you.

You restrained with some difficulty your desire to reply with a statement that would certainly condemn you to spend the rest of the afternoon in interrogation. Instead, you gently smiled, and when her eyes were no longer upon you, you expelled your impatience.

Not long after, there was the short notice coming from your Unit, announcing the end of the indoctrination. The window-wall behind the mentor darkened and the side walls of the room were lit with long lists of names, the Standings[3] of the one thousand Level Ten apprentices. Before granting permission to stand and leave, mentor Levine, herself standing next to the holoprojector, announced:

'For the next indoctrination, I shall begin the last topic of the year: a modern approach to the impact of the Torment in the surviving populations scattered across Artica. I remind you once more that fifty Credits are awarded to those who productively prepare and present it. Therefore, those of you who are intent on achieving this year's Highest Distinction award shall do well in preparing these final indoctrinations.'

From amongst the names and standings on the walls, fifty were highlighted in front of their respective number. You looked with indifference at your name in front of the number eight-hundred.

'According to the current Standings, apprentice Sophie Andersen, standing on the twenty-seventh, holds the highest standing of this class, followed by apprentice Heidi Lauren on the forty-sixth and apprentice Haji Donovan in the sixty-fourth. The lowest standings would do well to ask for some advice from these bright apprentices,' she said, glancing at you and some other apprentices who hung their heads in embarrassment.

She then nodded to the class, granting permission to stand up and leave.

You had barely risen from the chair when she added, 'Apprentice Balthazar, do refrain from leaving your seat.'

You let out a quiet sigh and sat down again, glancing at your colleagues as they rolled up their neuropads, packed them in their utility belts and walked past you. When Haji was leaving you caught his attention and whispered, 'Wait for me outside?'

'Certainly,' he said, bowing his head low in a display of solidarity.

When the last apprentice left and the sliding door behind you closed automatically, the room fell into an absolute silence. You remained in your seat, your head hanging low, your eyes fixed on the emptied desktop. You heard the mentor's footsteps approaching, echoing off the cold marble floor, and when the echoes suddenly stopped you raised you eyes to see her standing straight before you, her violet pants and jacket both tightly pressed against her tall scrawny body.

'Apprentice Balthazar, your behaviour throughout this year has expressed nothing more than your clear intent in confronting every mentor that calls upon your attention,' she started, and despite her apathetic stare, her voice was sharp. 'When it finally seems that you have caught interest in History doctrine, you seize the first opportunity I grant you to break the Directives and question the validity of your indoctrinations with, to say the very least, a slanderous insinuation.'

There was nothing you could say to amend your action, so you lowered your eyes and listened quietly.

'Not to mention your indecent act of defiance towards a mentor,' she said, and she was deeply disappointed when she saw you indifferent glance. 'What is the cause for such indiscipline? I would very much wish to know, for then I would be able to assist you in resolving your issues without being forced to notify the Council of Mentalists.'

Her warning ensnared your undivided attention. You straightened your back and gave her a solemn stare.

'This was my last admonition apprentice Balthazar. I earnestly advise you to fulfil your obligations as an apprentice, otherwise I shall have to fulfil a most unpleasant obligation of a mentor and fail you. You know very well the Council does not invest in lost causes. Consequently, a mentor does not invest in lost causes,' she calmly tugged at the hem of her violet jacket, clasped her hands in front of her waist and returned to her dull voice. 'As a means of recovering your lucidity, do perform the supplemental tasks that I shall be sending to your neuropad. Consider them a corrective measure as an alternative to Cognitive Rehabilitation[4]. Order ensures Progress, apprentice Balthazar.'

...any disobedience condemned without tolerance...every act of defiance punished without exception...

Outside the indoctrination room, the wide curved hallway was barely emptied. Most of the apprentices had already left and the only sound was the echo of footsteps. You walked down the stairwell and when you reached the ground floor, you headed towards the East entrance of the Academy where Haji chatted with Sophie. When you stopped before him, a troubled look on your face, he interrupted the conversation and asked with concern:

'Is everything well?'

'I think her patience is finally coming to an end,' you answered.

'I tried to caution you but I was unsuccessful. You were deeply asleep,' he explained.

You shrugged and smiled. 'It wasn't your fault,' you said. Then you mimicked mentor Levine, speaking in a tedious voice, 'apparently, she is not quite the admirer of apprentices who fall asleep during her dissertation regarding the greatness of our *illustrious* Guiding Father.'

'That and your eloquently put question,' Haji added, captivated by your mockery.

The ease with which you deliberately disrespected mentor Levine was bothering Sophie deeply, as was the way Haji fell under your misguided influence. She crossed her arms tightly and furrowed her thin golden eyebrows at you, 'Alan, have you realized that with the time you waste questioning everything that is indoctrinated you could be, the same way everyone else is, striving to achieve a high standing and ensuring your future as a citizen of Darm?' she prodded.

You buried your amusement under a stern face. It was unusual for her to scold you, but as you looked at her worried eyes, you rapidly realized she was merely attempting to express her concern about the negative influence you had on Haji.

'Sophie,' you said thoughtfully, 'our existence should not be limited to a standing that one can achieve by earning Credits, even less when those who grant them do so to keep us disciplined and obedient.'

Haji whispered close to your ear, *'Does that mean you do not mind arriving late and starting the race in last?'*

Suddenly, the reason why you had so eagerly waited for the end of the indoctrination popped into your mind.

'Shoot!' you let out the loud interjection and then scratched the back of your head, chuckling innocently.

Sophie squinted at you, 'Are you two going to break Directives again?' she asked, her voice a blend of concern tinged with reprimand.

'Something like that,' you answered, eyes lined with mischief.

She gave you a harsh stare. 'Some day the Council of Mentalists will not be as lenient with you as they have been until now Alan. And when that day comes, if I am to be interrogated by Overseers I shall say that I have nothing to do with any of you.'

'That is simply not possible,' Haji stated. 'You cannot lie without them knowing.'

She slapped her thighs, eyeing him with frustration, 'Haji, please be careful! We are one month away from becoming citizens. I do not want you to do anything to harm your citizenship.'

Haji looked into her amber eyes and spoke kindly:

'I would never do anything that would drive us apart Sophie.'

She was not expecting that comeback. Her cheeks slowly reddened and when she realized she was unable to restrain her embarrassment, her eyes fled to the transparent exit door, and then to your silly entertained expression. You quickly looked away in an effort to appear oblivious to their conversation.

She looked at Haji and gave him an endearing smile, 'And I appreciate your consideration,' she answered shyly, struggling to hold back her delight while her eyes glittered with joy. 'Now please be careful and take care of---him,' she said, pointing at you with displeasure.

Haji's remark had been by far his best attempt to reveal his interest in her, and he had eagerly waited for a reply that allowed him to safely confirm or deny that she was equally interested in him. However, her answer was not as revealing as he had expected.

He bowed and said soberly, 'I will Sophie.'

You and Haji were already stepping through the exit when Sophie remembered, 'Do not forget to show up at the East Retreat. We will be discussing the preparations for this year's Gathering.'

'I wouldn't miss it for all the Credits in Darm!' you answered loudly, drawing the attention of two apprentices exiting the Academy quite properly.

Sophie hid her face behind her long golden locks. 'One day I will be summoned to the Overseers. I can feel it,' she mumbled to herself, as she retreated to the broad study hall on the outer side of the curved hallway.

Second memory - Nightfall in the White Metropolis

[...] and the Academy for Indoctrination and Preparation for Citizenship. These will be the four facilities surrounding the Netcore, the primary structure of the metropolis. An ideal cylinder in shape, its semblance made entirely of a reflective composite, the Netcore shall reside atop the Central Circle and shall surpass in height and splendour any other structure ever built, rising above the storms as a symbol of our perseverance. Extending from the Central Circle along the cardinal directions, the Four Boulevards will stretch out to the Four Magnetization Towers. These structures shall emit a resonant magnetic field capable of providing inexhaustible energy through the known process of electrodynamic induction. Periodically installed along the rims of the Boulevards there shall be spacious platforms which will lift its inhabitants to the Panoramic Way. Spanning across the metropolis directly above the Four Boulevards, the Panoramic Way shall provide an alternative means of transportation. These will be the primary constructs of the prototype metropolis and they shall serve its inhabitants so that they may perform their duties in an efficient manner.

An excerpt from annex #21: Directives for the construction of Darm; Division of Planning under the authority of Mentalist Torval;

Outside the hallway, Mithras, the star that shone upon Artica and warmed its frozen crust, had already hidden behind the tall and imposing buildings of the Specialist Class Sector, engulfing the Academy in a fresh shadow. You rushed down the stairs and quickly crossed the main courtyard, adorned at the centre by a fountain with a white marble statue of the Guiding Father.

Upon entering the East Boulevard, you hastily weaved your way through the aligned flow of citizens as orderly as you could, climbing afterwards onto the nearest platform whose entrance remained perpetually guarded by two *sentinels*[5].

The warm maternal voice of Mother spoke in your mind: *"Access to platform number two authenticated and granted. Have a pleasant Rest Time, apprentice Balthazar."*

'I intend to,' you whispered to yourself as you stopped next to Haji in the back row of citizens.

The platform reached its maximum quota slowly, as citizens and apprentices returned from their tasks. By the look on some of their faces they were headed to their residences to find some well needed rest.

'Return hour...' you complained impatiently to Haji.

Haji nodded, smiling afterwards to the citizen in front of him, who had glanced back with an absent, tired face. Shortly after, the ascent was announced by the uncoupling of the magnetic locks that held it one step above the ground.

Five hundred meters above, you and Haji boarded a Panoramic Transport and took your seats. Apart from the flooring and the seats, which were made of a metal so polished that mirrored every passenger, the rest of the structure was made of *permaglass*[6], allowing for a panoramic view of Darm. Far to the East, beyond the countless blocks of residences and the Coastal Walkway, was the Sea of Tranquility.

'Sophie's really interested in you,' you said, sitting next to Haji in an aisle seat.

Sitting in a window seat and looking outside, Haji turned his attention to you and asked with enthusiasm, 'Are you for certain?'

You gave him a confused stare, 'Well, yes. She was practically speechless after you gave her that answer. And did you see the way she blushed?'

'Yes I did,' he said. 'But it seemed a normal reaction, given the circumstances.'

'A normal reaction?!' you asked, eyes widened in surprise. 'I can't understand how you see it that way.'

Haji stared at is boots absentmindedly while reviewing every nuance of her reaction, every detail of her bashful gestures, her glittering eyes, her coy smile, her mellifluous voice.

He sighed, 'It is hard to read her mind.'

'Haji, trust me. She likes you, *for certain,*' you jested, flashing a grin.

When you arrived at the Administrator Class Sector, you and Haji disembarked with many of the remaining passengers and entered the Sixth Platform. As it descended, you saw through the transparent platform the dense blocks of residences gradually grow under your feet. Darm was enduring the last weeks of the freezing winter of Artica, and the unrelenting snowstorms were still evident in the mantles of snow accumulated on the streets, fountains and rooftops.

Arriving at ground level, you and Haji stepped onto the street with hasty footsteps, and after a short walk you arrived at the crossroads that connected your streets.

'The first one to arrive at the meeting point waits for the other,' Haji reminded you. 'Stay out of trouble *rabble-rouser*!'

'You too *adjy,*' you quickly riposted, and as he turned to his street you turned to yours.

...what was the meaning of these names...

Whenever you were about to break Directives, you called each other by nicknames. Haji was the first to adopt them ten years before this time, after an act of insurgence at the Academy, where you attempted to instigate your fellow apprentices to skip indoctrinations. Haji was the only one to support you, and for that, both of you were deprived of Rest Day for the remaining of the year. He never blamed you for it, and he never left your side afterwards, regardless of all the trouble you got him into. It was long ago that the bonds of your friendship were first forged.

...Haji...what has become of you...

* * *

Before he could head for the Shelter, Haji had to deceive Mother by taking his routine path back to his residence. Mother was not only capable of accurately pinpointing the location of any darmian through the signal each Unit emitted, but also determining if that location was valid for their occupation. As an Apprentice, a journey to the Manufacturing Sector during Rest Time would be promptly characterized as inappropriate conduit.

As he crunched the layer of snow resting on the marble sidewalk, he remembered the day when the Shelter's owner gave him the program capable of eluding Her, and how he was able to re-route his Unit's signal by installing the program on his residence's *server*[7] and use the server as a bridge between his Unit and Mother. As a result, every time he activated the program he was free to travel to any sector of Darm while Mother saw him as simply an exhausted darmian lying on his bed.

When he arrived at his residence he greeted his caretakers, who were sitting on the comfortable sofa of the living room, and was delayed when he was forced to explain he was arriving late due to the meeting he had scheduled with his friends. After walking up the stairs to his room and activating the Signal Re-Router, he bowed to his caretakers and left quickly, seeming to his caretakers that he had only come to retrieve something he needed.

He then returned to the streets, trudging along the cold snowy pavement, his hands tucked in the jacket's pockets, his face hidden behind his facemask while his head tilted low beneath the green hood. He avoided proximity with other passersby, always keeping in mind he could not risk being identified.

...this was no memory of mine...

It was not indeed. All life is bound to the Tides of Fate, and as we flow through them we are free to see the course of events through the viewpoint of any life. It was your desire to see Haji that brought upon you a thread of his past.

...then I can control these visions...

You can, but only because your will is strong. However, you must take caution, for the journey through the Tides of Fate is not without peril to the unwary traveller. Its currents are treacherous and if your will falters you may lose hold over them and become trapped inside the life of another. As such, it is best that you restrain yourself from wanting to see more than what I have to show you.

***

After you activated your Signal Re-Router, you headed on to the meeting point, crossing the East Boulevard towards the first row of the tall large facilities of the Manufacturing Sector. When you arrived, you leaned against a *ventilation box*[8] and looked at the sky. Mithras had already sunk below the horizon, covering the heavens with shades of blue, which stubbornly forbade Oderon's Rings from claiming the night with their silvery light. Some of the largest lunoids already managed to shine through, and these stretched across the heavens from pale-blue twilight to dark-blue nightfall, their sharp glare preventing any other star from being seen.

Haji arrived soon after. He approached the ventilation box which spewed warm air into the atmosphere.

'It is a pleasant evening for a walk,' he remarked, his voice projected through the facemask. 'Did you go to bed?'

You stepped away from the box and greeted him with a bow.

'Something like that,' you answered in an amused tone, your face hiding behind the facemask as well. 'But Evander is becoming sort of a nuisance. He's trying to keep me up. I might just have to reprogram him.'

'For all the hardship you go through from having only one caretaker at least you have that commodity,' he stated.

You shrugged. 'I suppose. Shall we?'

He nodded.

The conventional way to enter any sector was crossing the checkpoints that connected the Four Boulevards with the streets and avenues of the adjacent sectors. However, each checkpoint was supervised by sentinels. Aware of the risk of being spotted by the droids, whose sensors were capable of detecting the incongruity of their signal, you avoided walking under the hovering lamps that lit the boulevard, hid from sight behind the benches and ventilation boxes, and then snuck inside the Manufacturing Sector through an unguarded alley between two facilities.

'Made it,' you said in a lively manner, after peering back and making sure no sentinels were marching your way.

Quietly treading towards the end of the alley, you entered one of the secondary streets only to quickly disappear from sight into the shadowy alley of the next row of facilities.

'I wonder if Brent has already prepared the interface,' you mumbled restlessly, as you reviewed the procedures for the race.

'That is not the worst of our concerns,' Haji whispered.

Despite his vague answer you understood what he meant to say. You knew as well as he did how complex and perilous it was to establish a connection abroad. Several dummy protocols were required to bypass the seemingly flawless control nodes that shielded Mother's communications network from unauthorized access. All that was needed for Mother to detect an anomaly and locate the source of the signal was but one of these protocols to fail. Every time you thought about it, you could not help but wonder why Brent risked his citizenship to grant you the opportunity to enjoy the best that Remgast had to offer.

Upon arriving at the alley adjacent to the facility concealing the Shelter, you stopped in front of its sealed maintenance door. You knocked once, stopped, and then twice.

Then you waited.

And waited.

Suddenly, the metallic door slid open.

From the barely illuminated interior stepped forth a tall imposing pyrean, broad in stature, with a stern face and strong chin that made him look older than he actually was. He was wearing a yellow jumpsuit packed with flap pockets, and his robust hands rested on a utility belt with several tools hanging from it.

He gave each of you a piercing stare, 'A little longer and I would have had Mother look for you,' he scoffed.

'You know how lengthy travelling can get during Return Hour, especially near the end of the year,' you explained.

'The actual truth is that Alan had another private conversation with the History mentor,' Haji stated.

You elbowed him, your eyes smiling innocently at Brent.

Brent pursed his lips and cautiously looked into the alley from one side to the other, 'Hurry inside,' he said, stepping aside.

You and Haji complied immediately and when the sliding door closed behind you, you removed your facemasks.

The facility was dark, except for a stream of light that stretched from an opened entrance atop a staircase to the right. A huge container loomed before you, blocking the access to the innermost part of the facility.

You followed Brent through the improvised corridor between the container and the steel staircase, 'So, Alan. You're trying to start an uprising?' he jested, looking back with a wicked grin.

You gave him a proud smile. Impressing Brent was the only award you cared about.

'Luckily for you I took the time to set up the interface,' he added.

Under the steel staircase was another staircase that led to the underground level. As soon as the luminous projectors lit up the pitch black basement, you followed Brent to a corner, walking past a circular platform whose function was to lower the cargo bundles onto the magnetic conveyor connected to the Materialization Chamber.

Stopping at the corner, Brent groped one flap pocket, and then the other, and another. He muttered some interjections and then looked at his utility belt. He fumbled in the belt's pocket and then pulled out his closed hand with a grin on his face, 'Almost forgot where I had put it. Almost,' he said.

In his right hand rested a smooth black cube the size of his palm. He turned to face the *fibreconcrete*[9] wall and kneeled. When he pressed the cube onto the wall with one thumb, the cube responded with a sharp *beep!* He then rose and stretched it diagonally across the wall. The cube was becoming a tall rectangular frame resembling that of a door, and when it seemed wide enough to be crossed, he pressed the thumb again. Almost immediately an image popped up from the wall inside the frame: a set of power bars filled in green with a message floating below, flickering with the word *"Ready."*

When Brent's finger touched the word, the casing emitted an ever higher shrill sound, and moments after, when the sound rose to a deafening screech, an intense flare erupted from the casing and converged into the centre in a blinding eruption of light that forced you to close your eyes.

Afterwards there was only a tenuous whirring, soft to the ears.

'Dive through,' you heard Brent say and you opened your eyes.

Diving through was the ideal expression to describe the passage through the liquefied wall, for the Matter Dispersion Device had converted the virtually impenetrable fibreconcrete into a viscous liquid. It was a process that required tremendous energy, but due to combined *electrodynamic induction*[10] the device was allowed to operate efficiently.

On the other side of the semi-transparent surface, leisurely undulating as if submerged, was a partial view of a scarcely lit room and you could see two barely perceptible armchairs with their backs turned against the opposite wall.

'I hate this part,' you complained.

Haji dived through first. His body plunged into the wall and emerged on the other side. Then he turned and smiled at you.

Brent stepped back, ushering you into the Shelter.

'Apprentices first,' he said, not on account of politeness you concluded by the grin on his face.

You threw him a grumpy smile and approached the wall. You plunged your right leg in and with your right foot you tapped the firm flat floor. Then you closed your eyes, held your breath and pushed yourself through, piercing through the hot layer of gel that thwarted your every movement only to spew you afterwards into the Shelter.

Third memory – When drifters race

[...] Remgast, the metropolis that hosts the drifter races and the only pyrean construct that matches the greatness and technological marvel of Darm. Although inviting apprentices to the Shelter does not directly justify the risk of exposing our entire operation, these games provide the apprentices a direct exposure to the reality outside of Darm which consequently helps gather supporters for the Uprising. When we have gathered enough supporters, we will set our plan into motion. We will begin by ***FILE CORRUPTED*** they were waiting for us in the tunnels. I don't understand how they found us. I cleared my mind from any thought. I made no ***FILE CORRUPTED*** our plan from the start. And now Vittas has killed Von Howitt and I am trapped inside an Air Intake Field. I won't make it through the night. They will come ***FILE CORRUPTED***

An excerpt from the captured log-files of the Silent Uprising; Division of Darmian Security under the authority of Mentalist Vittas;

The dimly lit chamber had a cosy appearance. It had a low ceiling, a fluffy dark-grey carpet and a row of six stuffed armchairs with their backs turned to six corresponding *holoscreens*[111]. Four of them were in suspension mode, displaying the Drifter Races's logo -

a mirrored D followed by an R blended in such fashion that seemed but one unusual symbol - while the two closest to the improvised entrance displayed a dark-blue background with silver lettered options, the start menu of Drifter Races. You rushed to the first armchair and sat down. Haji quickly followed, sitting on the other. Brent shuffled towards the far end of the chamber and let the weariness of a tiresome day sink him into the chair behind his desk. After rubbing his face, he put on the *neuroglove*[12] and activated the desk holoprojector atop the desk.

'Link yourselves to the *psysis*[13] and get inside the dream world,' said Brent.

You placed the mesh-shaped device on your head and laid back on the armchair as it reclined into a prone position.

'Have a nice dream,' he added.

You closed your eyes, your lips bearing a smile, and cleared your mind, allowing the dark quietness to lull you into a dreamless trance. Your emptied mind was soon lit by flashes of blurred images and garbled sounds; they came in increasing waves which began flowing like a smooth stream of water. Upon its surface, you saw the clear reflection of the game's options menu, with several options written in psychedelic-blue letters that floated freely over the water.

Amidst the silent dream, you heard the server's hostess, 'Establishing an uplink, please hold.'

Back in the Shelter, Brent was attempting to find the safest route for the uplink, steering his hand through the endless stream of data projected above his desk. He rushed along the floating green threads with unflinching concentration, dodging and avoiding every red cube before his path, letting experience guide his almost unconscious gestures with all the precision required for a flawless flight through the digital itinerary.

'This one looks safe,' he muttered to himself, pointing the index finger at a blue cube. 'Now, just a few dummy protocols and it's done.'

When he spread his fingers above the highlighted cube, it opened, exposing lines and lines of code impressed on each of the inner faces. He pointed to the face corresponding to the information packets sent to Mother and added a line that would bypass the protocols of the uplink with a dummy protocol containing uninteresting information, 'Through the duration of the race we shall be most enthusiastically delving into the records of past geothermal activity in the Sea of Tranquility. Nothing suspicious about it, nothing illegal,' he said to himself.

Alone in your dream, you configured the game options through a sub-menu filled with several parameters, touching the icons with one finger as if the dream had become a palpable reality where any object could be manipulated. Once the hostess confirmed that the uplink was established, you eagerly connected to the game server.

'Commencing translocation,' said the hostess.

The configurations menu evaporated in front of you and you fell at increasingly higher speed towards what seemed to be the upper view of a giant pavilion floating in dark space. It loomed and loomed ever closer, until you flew right through the ceiling and crashed on a small blue pad inside a vast white hall. You got on your feet, shook your head, and saw that you had arrived at the crowded Game Hall of the race rack. On the walls to your left and right were the tunnels that extended to the pits. At the end of the hall was the long check-in counter and right behind it was a window-wall with a view to the race track.

Haji was at your side on the spawning pad, clenching and loosening his fists and cracking his neck, left to right. You recognized him immediately although his face was not his own. Inside the dream world every user was able to customize his or her appearance through different criteria such as height, weight, hair, voice and even the colour and style of their race suits. It was since the very first drifter race that Haji chose to assume the shape of a short and chubby old pyrean, with plump cheeks and long gray hair. Though his was the shortest of all avatars participating in the drifter races, his limbs were so brawny that they had earned him the respect of every player, which was of great importance, for brawling was not uncommon outside the race track.

'Sturdy as ever,' he said looking at you, and his coarse voice was as warm as his merry smile.

Your avatar was of young age, tall and athletic with a fair noble countenance. Standing next to you, Haji was no higher than your hips and the two of you formed such a unique combination that you were easily recognizable to all your opponents. Rogli and Wogli was what they called you - yours being the first - and given that you were the only darmians playing the game, your nicknames were uttered with both humour and respect.

'Let's check-in,' you said and stepped down from the spawning pad.

Haji nodded and followed you.

Only one team of players remained in the Game Hall, and they stood amongst the crowd, seeming to be engaged in a heated discussion with four rowdy spectators concerning a lost wager. By the angry look on the spectator's faces it was evident that their patience was wearing thin. Gastians were lively people, and they seemed to find pleasure in engaging in silly competitions regarding just about anything that crossed their restless minds. When the two beleaguered players saw you, they found the perfect chance to leave with their pride - and their avatars – intact. As you walked past them, they greeted you cheerfully, briefly followed you, and then made a discrete run for the tunnel.

When you approached the counter and gave your nicknames, the two game administrators standing behind it, one plump the other gaunt, briefly halted their discussion on which of their avatars could wipe their nose with their toes. As soon as they confirmed your registration, they pointed to the tunnel that led to your pit and resumed arguing, without even glancing towards you. *'I'm* tellin' *ya* I can do it!' the plump one insisted, bouncing on one foot and pushing the other with both his hands.

You chuckled, and were about to step away from the counter when Brent's face popped up on the upper left corner of your *Field of View*[14], 'I am done here. The connection is untraceable and the dummy protocols are in place,' he said. 'I will be performing the maintenance I scheduled to avoid suspicion. Enjoy the race! I will be back once I am finished. Brent, away,' and his face popped out of sight.

Walking down the tunnel's bright blue rug, you could hear through every pressurized door the muffled sounds of drifters being powered up, the rattling of power drills, wrenches hammering on the ground and voices yelling at each other. At the end of the corridor you found your pit: *"Rogli&Wogli - Darmian Duo"* was written in psychedelic letters on a blue sign next to the metallic door.

The sliding door opened with a sharp hiss, releasing into the corridor a warm concoction of burnt fuel and sweat that had accumulated in the pit. You took a deep breath and allowed the stimulating smell to fill your lungs, 'The addictive smell of fun,' you said to Haji.

Then you rocketed towards your drifter, snatching the first neuroglove from atop a red tool cabinet, and pressing the drifter's canopy button. After it opened you jumped into the cramped cabin, whose interior was automatically lit by small cockpit lights. Lying in the ergonomic seat, you put on the neuroglove and began to calibrate the drifter to meet the racetrack specifications.

Haji entered calmly with short chubby steps, his boots glistening with the ceiling projector and clanging on the metallic floor as he walked past your drifter and stopped before his. It resembled a projectile with a large propulsion reactor in the back. Bulging just before its tip and nozzle were two ring-shaped rudders that allowed the pilot to manoeuvre it. Quietly admiring its simple design, he took his time to mentally review the calibrations he had devised.

'Last race we did relatively well,' you said from inside your cockpit. 'Up until the part I flew against Tzivo.'

'That was some explosion,' Haji answered. 'We definitely need to defend our approaches to avoid elimination if you are truly intent on reaching the top three this year,' he added, all the while setting up his drifter without the use of a neuroglove. It was a delicate task that required a tremendous abstraction from oneself, something you were not very good at, but Haji had become exceptionally proficient in interacting directly with dream worlds and using thoughts to alter them.

'Defending approaches would surely work against most teams,' you said, 'but not against Zig and Drom. They are just too good,' then you sighed, struggling to remember the rear ring-rudder calibration.

Haji's face popped up above your cockpit, his eyes glinting mischievously, 'If we are unable to avoid those two, I suggest we eliminate them.'

You stopped fumbling the neuroglove through the air and looked up at him, brows furrowed in doubt.

'Are you suggesting we race for elimination?' you asked.

'We most certainly will not,' Haji promptly replied. 'We will remain true to our goal and play for a clean victory. But I have a plan to turn their game against them. I want you to upgrade your drifter with reverse thrusters, and when I give you a signal, I want you to activate them.'

You contemplated his suggestion for a moment, 'You and your strategies,' you answered unconcernedly while accessing the drifter settings and clicking on the reverse thrusters icon. 'Very well, you've never let us down before.'

The countdown blinked and *beeped!* on a timer above the large access gate. Simultaneously, a game administrator calmly warned, his voice coming from a speaker next to the timer, *"All pilots are to lock inside their drifters. Opening gates in one minute."* Then his voice spiked before being cut off, *"I'm tellin' ya I can place my feet behind my head and still manage t'a---"*

Haji put his plump fingers in his gloves and his electric-blue helmet on his grey haired head, 'Enjoy the race,' he said before leaping into his drifter.

'You too,' you said.

You threw the neuroglove away, put on your helmet, and after the opaque canopy sealed you inside your drifter, pressurizing the interior with a soft whistle, the darkened cockpit slowly started to disappear, save for the handlebars and gauges. When it stopped, it had become practically invisible enabling you to see the pit all around it. Lying on the translucent seat, you looked down and felt you were floating above the metallic floor half a meter below.

After the pit was depressurized, the gate started to open and as it slowly rose to the ceiling, it unveiled a flat pit-lane with two parallel orange arrows flashing on a dark metallic pavement.

You powered up your drifter's engine and as it burned through the first injection of *liquid fuel*[15] you felt its thrust pull your body against the prone seat. The pavement slid below you, as you smoothly floated into the pit-lane. Looking to your right, you saw Haji's electric-blue drifter hovering alongside yours.

When you cleared your pit-lane and entered the starting line you were amazed by the spectacular view. Scattered throughout the dark background were galaxies of all sizes and shapes, and countless stars of white, yellow and red; the track itself orbited around a star system, its colossal star a blue giant being orbited both near and far by gaseous planets whose gravities had ensnared countless asteroids, round and lumpy. For every Championship and every track, the backgrounds were re-customized and re-rendered and for that reason you never ceased to be amazed by the endless variety of cosmic sights. This was one of the best you had ever seen.

"Race begins in five minutes," warned the admin's voice, stealing you from your awe.

The glare from the red starting-lights mirrored on the drifters' chassis hurt your eyes as you stopped on the starting-grid and studied the positions. On the qualifying session the week before, you had managed to achieve the third position while Haji achieved the fifth; had there not been a sudden connection failure and you were confident that you would have done better. Your heart pounded heavily when from the dark metallic pavement emerged ten pairs of magnetic locks that firmly clamped the drifters to their respective positions. Jets of burning fuel roared from the drifter's exhausts, clouding the space with plumes of red and blue.

"Opening general chat channel," said an admin through your helmet's headset.

In order to promote interaction between players a general communications channel was kept open for the duration of the race. Many used it to gloat when they performed a nice manoeuvre, but mostly it was used to taunt an opponent with whom a racer was fighting for a position. It was a dishonourable strategy to resort to psychological stress to win, but some players developed such a dreadful aptitude to eliminate opponents on account of provocations that it became a widely accepted and crowd-pleasing strategy.

The moment the channel was opened, a pair of menacing eyes behind the visor of a chromed red helmet projected itself on your *HuD*[16].

'Hello my not so fellow darmians. Ready to get your asses kicked, again?' said a voice with an unusual accent, the vowels strongly over-pronounced.

You sighed. You were never any good at answering Zigvirat's provocations.

Tzivo, a player from team *"Dun' look back!"* taunted, *'The only ass gettin' kicked is gonna be your, Zigvirat.'*

'Shuttup!' Zigvirat snarled. *'I ain't talkin' to ya. I's talkin' to our special guests.'*

Rist, Tzivo's teammate, threatened, *'Ya oughta watch y'er tone Zig, if ya wanna leave the game in one piece.'*

You stepped in unworriedly, 'Don't bother Rist.'

Zigvirat's eyes smiled scornfully and he mocked, '*Ah…so the pet can speak. I's starting t'a think your almighty daddy had forbidden that as well.*'

Haji suddenly intervened, '*If you are referring to our Guiding Father the answer is he has not. And I must inform you that any attempt of intimidation will invariably result in a needless waste of your concentration. This time we intend to finish the race, ahead of you.*'

Zigvirat's squinty eyes narrowed to the point of seeming closed, '*Ya betta not even try darmian, unless you want to be wiped out, prematurely.*'

Haji answered, '*If it comes to that I shall make certain that I take you with me.*'

Hovering in front of you, Zigvirat's chrome red drifter spewed irritated jet flames. '*That is what we shall see,*' he threatened in softly pronounced words.

"*Sixty seconds boys and girls!*" the admin warned with excitement; the general chat could be heard by every spectator, and as the provocations heated up they began to place their bets on the winner.

In the relative silence that followed Haji established a private connection with you, leaving it open so you could share private comments during the race:

'*Zigvirat and Dromuzit are going to control your approaches for certain,*' you heard his voice coming from behind his blue helmet. '*You must not let their taunting distract you.*'

Dromuzit, Zigvirat's overenthusiastic teammate, yelled through the general chat, '*PLLLACE YER BETS!!! Who's gonna be the first to turn into dust!*'

'*I will control the rear line,*' added Haji, a calm confidence in his voice. '*All you are required to do is prevent them from placing their drifters alongside yours.*'

Deadrun, from team "*Faster than U!*" riposted to Dromuzit's taunt, '*I gotta feelin' it's gonna be you. Ya gonna drift into the stars, headed for that one up there, the one yellow like ya teeth.*'

Zigvirat mocked, '*You just stay behind like you always do Deadrun.*'

"*Fifteen seconds!*" the admin warned.

'*I'M GONNA SMASH YOU TO BITS!!!*' yelled Dromuzit, letting out a hysterical laugh afterwards.

You answered Haji nervously, 'Easier said than done.'

"10, 9, 8…"

The potent combustion engines powered up to full throttle, buzzing vibrantly and spewing long torrents of blue fire that stretched several meters along the incandescent grids of the pavement. All across the starting lane, the drifters, whose colouring varied from matte black to electric green, had turned into unstoppable projectiles just waiting to be released from their magnetic locks. Inside your translucent cockpit the violent vibration was one jolt away from shredding your drifter to pieces, yet you smiled with joy, pulling the hem of your gloves before softly grabbing the handles next to your knees.

'May the best win,' you said to Haji through the private chat.

'May we be the best,' Haji answered.

"*...Three. Two. One!*"

The starting lights turned green, the magnetic locks retracted and the drifters instantly rocketed away with the sound of roaring thunders. The general chat was flooded with "*yeehaws!*" and euphoric laughter as trails of fumes were the only evidence left behind on the scorched starting grid.

Zigvirat swiftly stole the leadership from Rist on the first half-pipe, in a nerve-wracking overtaking that almost threw both of them out into the void as they rocketed around its edge. His teammate, Dromuzit, launched to fourth position and hastily encroached upon you as you struggled to tame your drifter, your hands tightly clenching the shuddering handles. In contrast, Haji had a soft start. He had lowered his drifter's burn to grant his position to a greedy opponent, and dropped down to sixth. You heard Malaq's ecstatic taunt through the general chat as he overtook him, spewing his exhaust over his path.

"The Space-Trash Grand Prize has begun," said the admin's voice through the loud speakers floating above the track. Immediately afterwards, a high tempo techno thump burst out loud, filling all players with an irresistible need for speed.

Although you were playing in vacuum conditions, visual and sound effects were added to the dream world, and these worked to the amazement of the spectators that watched the race behind the panoramic window of the Race Hall. The floating circuit had the shape of a giant 8 split into two symmetrical platforms separated by one hundred meters of empty space. The curves of the platforms formed an inclined half-pipe which straightened into four flat ramps that ended in two turbopads at the centre of the 8. The track had earned its title due to this intersection, for the turbopads boosted drifters to a treacherous flight that crossed trajectory with drifters coming from the perpendicular ramp. A simple miscalculation between two or more racers as they approached the turbopads could result in a collision that would instantly turn them into a dazzling shower of particles. These collisions led to the primary strategy for victory: Elimination, where a player would place their drifter alongside an opponent's and set their approach on a collision course with another drifter by pinning them down. It was a vicious strategy, but in drifter races it had become a source for excitement and spectacle, and ultimately, it came to define the purpose of the entire game.

As a result, by dropping down to sixth, Haji intended to form and lead the second line of drifters and ensure your safety by staying in front of the line and forcing the drifters behind to jump after you.

The first five laps were completed without significant events, even though some failed *ring-slaps*[17] activated the warning for Minor Collision on your HuD. Haji held the leadership of the rear line with ease: he sped along the half-pipes with a calm steadiness and foiled every one of Deadrun's attempts to place himself alongside him. Gradually, the positions were becoming consolidated, forming the two expected lines of drifters, and three laps later the distance between the two lines became far enough to allow eliminations.

In the front line, Zigvirat was maintaining the first position with unmatched skill, and he meant for everyone to hear his tireless taunts through the general chat, most of them aimed at Rist, who was desperately trying to overtake him.

You ignored his provocations, as you were entirely focused on preventing Dromuzit's relentless attempts to slap your rear rudder; you knew that if he succeeded you would be in trouble, for Dromuzit's bold configuration favoured speed over stability and his plan quickly became evident: once he disabled your ring-rudders he would place himself alongside your drifter and control your approaches. But a simple plan is often a predictable one, so you devised the best way to counter it. You took advantage of your drifter's balanced configuration to maintain the right angle along the half-pipes, and using the rear view display on your HuD you continuously blocked Dromuzit's drifter whenever he entered the stretch for the ramp.

'Turn on the collision alarm. Eliminations are about to begin,' you heard Haji's voice through the private channel.

Zigvirat was the first to control Rist's approach. On the beginning of the nineteenth lap, he turned his game against him by placing his drifter in front of Rist's and lowering his speed, forcing him to either match his speed or attempt an overtake. Rist was so eager to claim first place that he saw it as an opportunity and accelerated to full throttle. After the tight half-pipe, the stretch for the ramp came into Rist's view. He was side-by-side with Zigvirat when the approach began, but no matter how hard he pressed the pedal, he could not manage to overtake him, for Zigvirat had favoured speed in his configuration and could easily match Rist's.

"Collision imminent!" flashed red in Rist's HuD, foretelling his fate, but he would not let himself be intimidated by his hated opponent: if he were to be eliminated, he would make sure Zigvirat would blow up with him. So he answered his taunt daringly and fell into his trap. The first drifters of the second line - Haji's included - furiously drifted through the space in front of them. In the last instant, side-by-side in full flight Zigvirat - who had until then been holding back – pushed into full throttle and sprang gloriously ahead

of the trajectory of the remaining drifters coming from the perpendicular ramp.

'BOOM!' Dromuzit yelled in general chat, just before the space between the ramps burst in an intense flash that blinded all who dared to watch.

"Multiple collisions!" warned the admin's voice through the loud speakers.

'Alan, report,' Haji requested.

'I'm here!' you answered, trembling with excitement. You had blindly drifted through the blast and landed almost out of luck on the platform ahead.

"Players eliminated: Rist, Tzivo, Brady; The "Dun' Look Back!" team has been eliminated," said the admin, followed by a wave of applause and cheers that poured out of the loud speakers. Zigvirat and Dromuzit added their voices to the cacophony, flooding the general chat with gloat and mockery.

'Zig managed to eliminate three players in one approach!' you said with both astonishment and dread through the private channel. 'And now I'm between him and Drom. Haji you better put your strategy into motion real quick because I'm next!'

'For now you just have to prevent them from setting up your approach,' was his calm answer.

'That's easier said than done!' you cried.

You struggled to remain calm while tirelessly steering both handles to coordinate the ring-rudders, holding the unstable equilibrium between positioning and velocity that allowed your drifter to remain permanently in front of Dromuzit's.

During the next five laps, Deadrun and Malaq were eliminated on account of a slight miscalculation from Deeda, Malaq's teammate and the only female player in the competition. She had accidentally blinded him just before the turbopad by crossing her drifter's exhaust in front of him. Malaq had only an instant to yell at her before turning into a spectacular shower of particles. She apologized through the general chat, even though her teammate's avatar was reduced to dust.

'I couldn't have done it better, Deeda,' mocked Zigvirat who had watched the approach by looking straight upwards in one of the inclined half-pipes.

Only half the players remained at the start of the three final laps. You were still following Haji's request and trying your best to prevent Dromuzit's attempts to control your approach, but you were gradually becoming outplayed by both your opponents, who coordinated their drifters to encroach on you from both ends.

On the second row, Haji kept Deeda safely under control.

'You are doing well,' he spoke to you in a supportive manner. *'We are nearing our move.'*

'It's about time you told me your plan! I'm starting to get tired!'

'And they are becoming overconfident,' he remarked. *'Only two laps remain before the finish. They will try everything to Eliminate you before the end, and when they do, I want you to let them.'*

'That's your plan?!' you cried. 'Hold out until the final lap only to let them eliminate me before the finish line? I might as well give up now!'

'Stay calm, that is not going to happen,' Haji reassured. *'I just want them to think they have you, right to the last moment, just before the last jump. But when I give you the signal, you activate the reverse thrusters.'*

For a second you tried to imagine the outcome of the move; and a second was all the time Dromuzit needed to position his drifter at your right side. When he did, Zigvirat quickly reduced his speed and slid down to your left side. You barely had time to realize what had happened before you were trapped between both of them.

'Caught in a clinch,' said Zigvirat's pleased voice through the general chat.

Then they both began *pinching*[18] your drifter, smashing it once, and twice, and thrice. A torrent of sparks sprayed from the electric-blue hull and glittered into space.

'Hey Drom, Lookey here! A fidgety darmian!' – Zigvirat yelled, and again he smashed his drifter against yours; the crowd cheered when your front ring-rudder was torn from your drifter and floated away into space.

'OOPS!' yelled Dromuzit. *'That had to be important!'*

'I've lost all frontal steering,' you warned Haji.

'Let them control your approach,' he replied. *'It is time to put our plan into action.'*

Haji discretely began to lower his speed, allowing Deeda to move in and overtake him. Once she was alongside him, speeding up to pass, Haji quickly matched her speed and their drifters darted furiously side-by-side towards the turbopad. Zigvirat and Dromuzit saw the dangerous wall that had formed on the perpendicular lane and they pressed down on your drifter to block your escape. Instead of breaking, you did not make any effort to avoid them.

'Submitting already, huh?' Zigvirat asked and his voice seemed almost disappointed. *'Being a nice boy like your daddy taught you!'*

'LOSER!' cried Dromuzit. *'At least put up a fight!'*

They pinched your drifter with theirs and began setting your approach on an interception course with the two drifters climbing up the ramp on the other platform. Deeda buffeted Haji's drifter until the last moment, attempting to intimidate him and force him to break, but Haji stayed on her side with undisturbed serenity. When her attempts failed, Deeda set up his approach to intercept your drifter's trajectory.

You sprang into space and your drifters whizzed past each other, avoiding collision by a mere strand of hair before all five drifters landed harmlessly on their respective platforms. The race continued to the sound of awe of the spectators.

'DAMN LUCKY!' yelled Dromuzit through the general chat.

Haji was not impressed, nor did he consider it to be luck, for he had calculated everyone's trajectory down to the millimetre.

"It's the Final Lap!" announced the admin above the thrilled cheers, and the excitement was justifiable for they had not seen such an exciting Space-Trash finale since the dawn of the game.

As they entered the half-pipe, and with their drifters' hulls upgraded to withstand damage, Zigvirat and Dromuzit pinched your drifter without concern, and in an outstanding stunt, Zigvirat tilted his drifter across the lane and with a short thrust he picked your front ring clean with the tip of his drifter, resuming his course afterwards without even lagging behind.

"Steering disabled. Hull in critical condition," the red warning flashed intermittently in your HuD.

'Hang in there!' you pleaded to your drifter, in response to the ominous sounds of cracking and tearing coming from just about every part of its outer shell.

The final stretch came into Haji's sight; rays of the giant blue star shimmered on his electric-blue drifter as he started his final approach, hard-pressed against Deeda's electric purple drifter.

'Get ready to activate the reverse thrusters,' you heard him through the private channel.

It was the final jump for the remaining five. The Game Hall was teeming with fervent spectators, some with their eyes fixed on the visual projectors others cramming against the wide window that stooped over the track. On one platform Zigvirat and Dromuzit were overjoyed: they had neutralized your drifter and their victory was soon at hand. On the other, Deeda was struggling to overtake Haji: she would mend her mistake and finish the race in first even if she had to Eliminate all her opponents.

Haji was relying on just that and he effortlessly carried out his plan, matching his speed as both darted side-by-side up the ramp.

"Collision imminent!" the red caution flashed on the upper view of every player's HuD.

As you came up the ramp to the final jump, Zigvirat and Dromuzit pointed your drifter towards Haji's and Deeda's. Your approach had been too easy to set up. You heard Dromuzit's laughter in the general chat.

The turbopad's edge approached menacingly fast, your drifter was smashed against theirs, and when the boundary was almost upon you, in that last split-second before the edge, time slowed down and all your senses kindled to their fullest. The sound of the drifters roared on your ears; your heart pounded in your chest; you felt the slow tempo of the techno beat resonating through all your avatar as the smell of burnt fuel flooded your nostrils and you heard Zigivirat's mocking aloud on the general chat:

'So long sucka!'

'Now,' you heard Haji's calm voice.

You activated the reverse thrusters with Zigvirat and Dromuzit still pressing you. Out of instinct Zigvirat stopped pressing and hit full throttle, springing into space in a safe trajectory. On the other hand, Dromuzit was still laughing maniacally when his drifter veered to the left and was boosted aimlessly towards a star as yellow as his teeth.

Eyes shut tightly, Deeda crossed ahead of Zigvirat while Haji pointed his drifter towards Zigvirat's. Full throttle into the flight, Zigvirat could only but stare in dismay as the nose of Haji's drifter flew straight towards his flank. He yelled before being cut off, *'Son of a—'*

A silent blinding light filled the entire race track.

"Multiple collisions!" yelled the admin's voice as an eerie silence overcame the entire audience.

The space between the ramps burst into a thunderous explosion that outshone every star and galaxy just as two drifters landed safely on the platforms, unleashing a deafening ovation that would have blown the speakers away if they were real.

"Players eliminated: Zigvirat, Dromuzit, Wogli; How about that, the "Eliminators" have been Eliminated!" said the admin's voice above the deafening noise.

The coruscant light slowly faded, unveiling a massive shower of dazzling particles that rained down on the entire track for minutes, many even floating far beyond like shooting stars falling into the void. The sight was a magnificent reward granted to the two drifters that crossed the finish line and a wall of light that burst into sparkling fireworks.

"We have a winner! Wogli from the team Darmian Duo! Second place goes to our deeeellectableee Deeeeeda from the team Metal Kitty! All remaining players eeeliminated!" yelled the admin.

'*YEAAA!*' you shouted inside your drifter, your avatar trembling with excitement. 'We did it!'

You savoured the moment with a victory lap on your tattered and steerless drifter, trundling it along the half-pipes and allowing their curvature to lead you along the track. After the seemingly endless applause subsided into cheerful murmuring you exited the track with the *"Return to pit"* command. Both your drifter and your *avatar* disintegrated, leaving behind an empty, battered, scorched track.

Back on the pit, Haji was waiting for you. After you emerged from the *Avatar Rematerialization and Matter Translocation Pad*[19], encircled with twirling specks of light, he greeted you with a low bow.

'I assume congratulations are in order,' he said.

'Did you plan this from the beginning?!' you asked with amazement as you stopped before him.

'Not quite,' he answered, knowing the time had finally come to reveal his plan, 'I did not mean to collide with Zigvirat. I intended to force his elimination with Deeda but when you lost both ring-rudders I realized that my plan would not succeed. So as an alternative, I allowed Deeda to skid past me at the turbopad, thus preventing Zigvirat and Dromuzit's attempt to direct you towards us, and then I flew against Zigvirat, thus preventing him from achieving victory. Furthermore, I was confident that you would manage to eliminate Dromuzit even without steering, which you eventually did, and since you were ahead of Deeda my sacrifice ensured your victory.'

You only understood half of what he said, with the excitement rushing through you. But his strategy had been so effectively implemented that you asked, 'Have you ever considered overthrowing Gadim and becoming Darm's Guiding Father?'

...and what a Guiding Father you would have been...I would have followed you to The End...

Haji shrugged and smiled, 'It is not a role I wish to perform,' then he pointed towards the airtight door that led to the corridor. 'Come, it is time to claim your reward.'

Outside the pit, a loud commotion was coming from the Race Hall at the end of the tunnel, and its entrance seemed congested with players and spectators sharing in laughter and conversations. As you approached, your path was suddenly blocked by the *"Eliminators"*. They stared at you with stern faces, their eyes kindled with anger. Their avatars were practically identical: tall, bulky and ridiculously brawny, giving the peculiar appearance that their tight red tracksuits were one size too small. Their faces were almost entirely tattooed and their hair was flaxen, short and curly; their facial bone structure was overly protruded, leading you to assume they had made a terrible miscalculation when creating their avatars and were not aware of the *"undo"* command. They narrowed their eyes and Zigvirat greeted you, his facial muscles filled with tension, 'In Remgast we have a saying. Only a coward upgrades their drifter with reverse thrusters.'

You stood your ground staring at him defiantly, your avatar slightly less imposing than his. From the tension that followed you were almost certain that a brawl was about to start. But just as you were about to punch him in the face in a pre-emptive attempt to finish him quickly, he suddenly bowed, hesitantly at first.

'Congratulations for the victory,' he snarled between gritting teeth.

He raised his head and eyed Haji with contempt, 'Wogli, your move was unexpected. It seems that you are beginning to learn the purpose of this game. It's about time.'

'It is only a matter of knowing your opponent,' Haji answered, adding a courteous bow, 'besides, you should have suspected. I warned you that if I were to lose you would lose with me.'

Zigvirat sneered, 'Even if I lost, you lost too, and *yer* teammate only eliminated Dromuzit with luck.'

'I am not surprised that you think that way,' said Haji. 'The highest precision in calculating an approach may pass as luck to the untaught mind.'

It was clear that Zigvirat was trying to understand his statement. His frowned face twitched, his eyes stuck in an empty stare, revealing the enormous intellectual effort that was taking place. Then, as he finally grasped the meaning, he loomed his tall muscled avatar over Rogli's short chubby avatar, 'Are *ya sayin'* I'm stupid? How about I smack your ass back to your daddy and teach you how we solve things in Remgast?'

The crowd nearing the entrance to the hall formed a half circle around you. A fight was always the perfect way to end a race and some of them started chanting repeatedly, *"Brawl! Brawl! Brawl!"*

Suddenly Brent's stern face popped up in front of your FoV.

'Time is running short,' he said with unease. *'If you start a fight I'll have to pull you out. Go get your cup instead.'*

Immediately after, you stepped in and gently pushed them aside.

'Calm down Zigvirat, this is only a game,' you said, calming yourself down as well. 'We're here to have fun, not to break teeth or bones, real or not.'

'Says the pompous winner that wants *t'a* fetch his prize,' Dromuzit added with a crazed grin.

Zigvirat frowned at you, leaned back, and poked Haji's head with one large index finger, 'You're lucky your *buddy* stepped in.'

'Once more, it was not luck,' Haji calmly answered. 'I knew he would, even though he did not have to.'

Zigvirat tossed his hand in the air, '*Bahh*...I'm not *wastin'* my time with your kind,' then he glowered at Haji. 'Be it gastian or darmian, you *telepaths* are all the same arrogant *bastards*.'

He turned his back and walked into the crowd, leaving you and Haji behind, blinking at each other.

'What did he say?' Haji asked, utterly confused.

'The *telepath* part or the *bastard* part?' you asked.

'Both.'

You shrugged, 'We should ask Brent.'

Haji nodded, 'Let us get your cup before that,' he said and trotted into the Race Hall, leading the way through the dispersed crowd.

Moments later you were surrounded by the cheering mob: there were the players, still wearing their race suits, the tall and short game administrators, who were still discussing about feet and noses and ears, and many spectators who had watched the race and were now forming a circle around Deeda. Once the winners were formally announced, you and Deeda stepped up to the podium that had taken the place of the counter in front of the panoramic window and the administrators handed the cups to both of you. They were simple in concept: a flat and round bottom and an arm-shaped bar, yours crafted in diamond and Deeda's in gold, but on top of the bar was a wide open hand holding a transparent spherical orb, and inside the orb was a miniature Space-Trash racetrack, endlessly replaying the race with its miniscule drifters racing about its eight shaped circuit and jumping in space from platform to platform. Occasionally, a flash of light would erupt from it.

Then the skinny admin spoke, as if reciting a rehearsed speech, 'These Dream Cups represent the Awards for this year's Champions of the *Space-Trash Grand Prize*. They will forever remain in display in the trophy stands of your pits,' then he added as a joke. 'Don't let the dust settle!'

Loud applause filled the hall. Deeda lifted her cup and pointed it to Malaq, screaming repeatedly, *"This one is for you baby!"*

You lifted your cup and let out a truly pleased smile. Standing before so many unknown gastians who lauded you without reserve was an overwhelming sense of accomplishment. It was the first cup you had won, and you owed it to you teammate and best friend.

...happiness...I had forgotten how good it feels...

'And now's the time to *partaaay*!' said the chubby admin, and when he clapped twice the hall's walls and ceiling disappeared, granting an outstanding view of the starry space.

You climbed down from the podium and presented your cup to Haji; he received it with a smile on his face. Almost immediately afterwards you crossed the crowd of gastians and entered the spawning pad. You looked back, already regretting having to leave, and took some time to cherish that last moment, where you saw and heard everyone enjoying themselves. With sparkling chalices in their hands, whose liquid contents twirled and rippled like a miniature-whirlpool, many chatted amusedly, others gazed at the stars and galaxies and others watched the highlights of the race, replayed by holographic drifters racing around the racetrack. Deeda was chatting with one of the administrators next to Malaq, who was showing off their golden cup to everyone. Then, leaning on a wall, were Zigvirat and Dromuzit, looking back at you with a peaceful smile. Zigvirat lifted his chalice towards you and drank in your homage.

'It's been a pleasure, Rogli,' said Zigvirat, and his voice was now kindly.

'Until our next race,' you answered and grinned wickedly.

You had already realized that his tough and rough attitude was just for show and intimidation. Deep down, he was just like you: a friendly young pyrean trying to enjoy his existence the best he could and having fun doing so.

'If only I could stay…' you whispered to yourself.

And your avatar vanished from that place, never to return again.

You slowly opened your eyes, a bittersweet smile on your face. You leaned forward and greeted Brent who congratulated you and complimented Haji for the cunning plan that had earned you the victory. He had watched the end of the race on the holoscreens behind your chairs and was absolutely delighted with the outcome. After powering down the server and crossing the liquefied wall that separated the Shelter from Darm, he and Haji continued the conversation with enthusiasm:

'I lost count on the number of times you were close to being Eliminated!' he said.

'It was an intense race,' Haji stated, a simple smile on his face.

You were quietly following them behind, your attention focused inward, and in the ensuing silence you suddenly asked, 'Brent, what's a telepath?'

Walking up the stairwell, Brent tripped on one step but quickly regained his balance.

'And a bastard,' Haji added.

Arriving at the ground floor of the facility, he stopped and frowned at both of you, 'Those are some of the things you're not meant to know,' he said sternly.

'Can we ask the gastians?' you said.

'No,' he promptly answered. 'This was the agreement when you joined the Shelter.'

You nodded, giving him an absentminded stare.

After the maintenance door was tightly sealed behind, you carefully trudged through the cold streets of the Manufacturing Sector. A clouded night was settling over Darm and a chilling breeze hissed through the nooks of the factories. Rest Time was all but spent and the streets were utterly silent.

Hiding in the alley between the two last facilities before the East Boulevard, Brent took his leave with a discrete bow, 'Go through the cloisters and stay out of sight.'

You and Haji nodded.

He was about to step into the Boulevard when he turned back, 'One last thing. The Shelter is going to be closed for a couple of days. I'll let you know when you can come back.'

'Will it be open by the time of the next race?' you asked with concern.

He shrugged, his hands in the pockets of his jacket, 'I can't say.'

You were not convinced that he was uncertain and you felt that he was trying to keep himself from explaining the reason.

He looked at the dismay in your face and rubbed your hair with his big hand, 'Don't worry. I won't forget about your race,' he said and grinned wickedly.

'You better not!' you replied, grinning back.

'Well, today was fun. Be safe,' he said and walked on alone, across the luminous warm Boulevard that separated the two sectors.

...he was a good friend...

He was more than that, as you will come to remember. He always tried to catch as much of your races as he could despite having to perform the extraordinary maintenance. The first race he ever saw you play was an exciting memory he remembered with nostalgia, even if you and Haji had suffered an utter defeat. With some pride, he would consider himself your game mentor and he often offered you suggestions for bold and daring moves. He very much enjoyed talking with you after the races and he cherished every moment of joy he could share with you for he felt he was giving you the opportunity to enjoy life as it was meant to be enjoyed.

...he bore the fate of those who are born to follow...yet he found a path of his own...

After a short disquieting stroll that felt too long, you and Haji arrived at the crossroads that led to your residences. You were weary but pleased.

'Have a nice rest and see you tomorrow at the Academy,' you said before leaving.

'Are you forgetting the meeting?' Haji asked just as you turned to leave.

You let out a sigh through the facemask - you had forgotten about it. You were so pleased with the victory that you felt that your tiresome day had come to a suitable ending. All you wanted now was the quiet comfort of your room.

You threw him a weary scowl, 'Do we really have to? I'm tired and I still want to look into some things in the *Database*[20].'

'Well I told Sophie I was going, so I have to,' then he added with a pleased voice,' and I want to. As for you, you would do well to come. Cathy will be assigning tasks for the Gathering and your presence is needed.'

You probed your mind to read the time given by your Unit: Dinner Time was coming soon and if you were to go, you would have to go now.

'All right,' you sighed and added discretely, 'I'll go let Mother know I'm back on my feet. Meet you here in ten minutes?'

'Certainly,' Haji said before bowing and parting in the opposite way.

Fourth memory – At the East Retreat

Even though social interaction was irrelevant to the accomplishment of the metropolis' purpose, the Pyre's social heritage demands that darmians be granted the possibility to engage in such activities. As a result, four public establishments shall be built at convenient locations and equipped with all the necessary commodities. These Retreats, as they will be named, shall be available after Work Time and they shall grant the darmian a place to fraternize without supervision, the sole requirement being that they follow the Directives for social interaction. Although optional, their implementation is strongly advised, for all preliminary experiments reveal an increase in productivity of twenty percent on the experimental group, as opposed to the control group, which when deprived of social interaction revealed a decline of thirteen percent in productivity and an increase in suicide rates.

An excerpt from Annex #15: Extraordinary contingencies; Division of Darmian Affairs under the authority of Mentalist Silas;

You and Haji arrived at the East Retreat a while into Dinner Time. It was an out-of-the-way establishment, encompassing the entirety of the base of the gigantic East Magnetization Tower. Snow had started to fall, and as you walked along the retreat's round window-wall, you saw through the shaded permaglass several pairs of citizens and apprentices sitting and chatting inside many booths. Sophie was there, inside one of the booths. Cathy and Jack were there too, sitting across the table from her. Ever since the start of apprenticeship did your feelings for them grow. Now, gazing at them from outside the window, it came to you how fond you had become of your friends and the more you thought about what they meant to you, the more the desire to rest vanished.

The cuddled entrance was facing the sea and had a luminous sign above it with the holographic words *"East Retreat"* tinting the snow with shades of green.

Entering the round antechamber, you sloughed off the thin layer of snow from your green uniform, and once the temperature matched the warm twenty degrees inside the retreat, the round door blocking your path slid into the wall. You entered the acclimatized hall, approached the broad counter at the centre and greeted Colt, its administrator. He did not pay you much attention, seeming rather immersed in his customary task: watching the weekly bulletin displayed on one of the holoscreens attached to the large central pillar while mindlessly cleaning a spotless cup with a stainless cloth.

'Saluta---' you said, but Colt immediately raised a finger in front of his lips, his eyes turned to the holoscreen.

You leaned over the counter and Haji leaned at your side and all three watched the weekly bulletin. It was being presented by a female darmian with a tidy appearance and straight brown hair pulled behind her ears. Her voice was clear and soft:

"On Vanguard research station, progress with the research conducted on the immunization of single cell organisms has reached an unprecedented breakthrough. After extensive manipulation of genetically modified cells, Project Specialists succeeded in reversing the mutations caused by the retrovirus PIn-T2. Result analysis suggests that this process can be replicated, and Specialists are confident that the research is close to eradicating the retrovirus from the Pyre genome. Our Guiding Father grants us his words on the subject:"

On the holoscreen emerged the elder countenance of Gadim. His short white hair was combed backwards and his hazel eyes had a kindly smile. He spoke with a mellow albeit firm voice, seeming that all his years of life had done nothing to spoil his vigour, granting him unparalleled resolve instead.

"This revolutionary achievement serves to demonstrate our commitment in achieving Darm's purpose. It serves to acknowledge Darm as the most advanced society of the Pyre, and acknowledges as well the efficiency of the Council's Guiding Principles. Citizens and apprentices of Darm, we are nearing the end of the suffering that has devastated the Pyre since the dawn of the Age of Obscurity.

As your Guiding Father, I commend you for your vital efforts in upholding the standards of our metropolis. Order ensures Progress."

His face disappeared and the speaker moved on to less important reports.

Haji looked at you, 'It appears that your caretaker has made significant progress with the research,' he said.

The statement sparked Colt's curiosity. He halted his compulsive cleaning and looked at you, his dark eyes widened in expectation.

'It appears indeed,' you answered, tapping the counter, letting slip an embarrassed smile, dividing your attention between the two pairs of eyes. When their silent gaze became an off-putting stare you added, 'I don't know anything! She doesn't tell me anything!'

Your answer drowned Colt's curiosity. With one swift turn of the head he returned to his endless task of rotating the cup with one hand and scrubbing it with the other.

You did not bother to bid your leave to him. You and Haji stepped away from the counter and headed down the corridor across the circular rows of booths. Most of them were occupied by weary citizens, others by apprentices engaged in conversations behind a transparent soundproof dome. At the southernmost end of the establishment you found Sophie, Cathy and Jack - they seemed to be in a cheerful mood. Once Sophie saw Haji, she found room for you to sit. The round booth was composed of one cushioned bench coated with a red hued fabric and a circular table crammed in the middle. You sat nearest to the retreat's window while Haji and Sophie sat next to you. Cathy and Jacky remained seated at the opposite side.

Jack smiled at you and spoke in a self-satisfied tone, 'Great intervention today Alan. Tell us what happened after we left. Did mentor Levine invite you to a private indoctrination in her residence?' he asked sarcastically.

You looked at him and smiled. You had not just won a drifter race to let yourself feel intimidated by your friend's taunt, 'You know how it goes. Some are born with charm, some work hard to get it.'

Jack combed his dense blond hair with one hand, his lips casting a smile as big as his face, 'You are right on that one,' he said. 'But you are not doing that bad. And if you need some hints you know you can count on me.'

Cathy gave him an incredulous stare, 'He was talking about you Jacky. What he meant to say is that *he* is the one born with charm.'

You chuckled, while Sophie and Haji remained oblivious to the conversation - they were sharing intimate smiles and speaking quietly with one another.

'So you want to compete then?' Jack answered, his brows furrowing defiantly above his light-blue eyes. 'I hope you realize that you are no match for my persuasive nature.'

He leaned back in the seat and sprawled his arms, wrapping one around Cathy's slender shoulders - she turned her head and flared her nostrils seeming that she had smelled something unpleasant.

'You'd lose,' you objected, widening a grin.

Cathy pushed Jack's arm aside and chimed in, 'Please behave. There are girls here, or did you forget?'

Jack looked at Cathy with a false look of guilt, 'We were just kidding. Alan knows it. Right?' he asked, glancing at you.

You smiled, 'All I know is that I'm going to order something. I'm starving,' you said, your answer more directed at the rumbling in your stomach that at Jack.

'I will order as well,' Haji intervened, interrupting his conversation with Sophie.

Lying flat on the centre of the table was a holoscreen displaying an in-depth menu of the establishment. You logged in to the server by waving you forearm over it and using Thought Interaction you ordered your desired food: two nutrient bars and a vitamin shake. After taking your order, the holoscreen slid into the table, and your order was raised on top of a tray from the opening. You picked up the tray and the holoscreen slid to its place with the notice *"Have a pleasant meal."* floating inside it.

After Haji ordered and received his meal, the thin dome-shape curtain lowered over the booth, enclosing you and your friends inside it. Then the calm and tranquilizing voice of Mother spoke, *"Please select a theme."*

'Tropical sea!' shouted Sophie above Cathy and Jack; you could not care less as you chewed on one of the nutrient bars.

"Theme selected: Tropical sea. Have a pleasant Dinner Time," Mother added.

'*Aww*...again Sophie?!' complained Cathy, softly banging her head on the table and then pushing her curly red hair aside as she looked at Sophie, 'Next time it is my turn!'

Sophie's auburn eyes brightened and she nodded joyfully.

As if it had become a live painting, the dome-shaped curtain turned into a sand filled beach encircled by an endless ocean with a clear blue sky above. The sparkling waves calmly embraced the shores in relaxing comings and goings, wetting the glittering sand.

Cathy scowled, as the relaxing sound of waves washed over the booth accompanied by a calm breeze. Then, she began, 'Now that we are all here, it is time to get started. As you all know, five weeks from now we will no longer be apprentices. For that reason, I proposed the Council of Mentalists that this year the Gathering take place in my suite, and earlier this morning my caretakers and I received the authorization from Mentalist Silas.'

Scraping the bottom of your empty cup with a straw, you gazed at Cathy with curiosity. Mentalist Silas was the Head of Darmian

Affairs and would not have allowed a Gathering to take place in a private habitation under normal circumstances.

'That is great!' cheered Jack.

'Will any Council representatives be attending?' Haji asked.

'Yes,' answered Cathy. 'One of the conditions imposed by Mentalist Silas is that we are to be supervised by Acolytes.'

The bubbling echo coming from your cup went silent.

'That is not so great,' said Jack, hanging his head.

'Well it was either that or having the Gathering at the Academy as is customary,' Cathy added.

As you listened, you could not help but feel frustrated that the gastians had the liberty to entertain themselves without any supervision, while darmians could not even have a formal event in a private suite without the Council of Mentalists prying into it. You put down your vitamin shake and before you gave it any thought you complained, 'This isn't right. The Council treats us like we're still infants. We obeyed every Directive this year and we can't even celebrate our turn to citizenship without having to be supervised?'

The answer came from Sophie, 'Alan, Mentalist Silas is opening an unprecedented exception and in return all he demands is that our Gathering be supervised. What more can you ask?'

Cathy added kindly, 'It is only understandable Alan. Mentalist Silas demands supervision simply to ensure our safety. Our Guiding Father is a great visionary who created this metropolis to help the

Pyre and the Mentalists are doing a remarkable effort in maintaining it in order.'

Sophie scolded, 'And if you had been more attentive to Demography and History doctrines you would know that every pyrean outside Darm is struggling for their mere survival against the Torment and against the harsh environmental conditions. Our Guiding Father has saved us from all this.'

...ignorant trusting fools...

You knew for a fact that for the very least Remgast was a place where neither the Pyre's genetic flaw nor the cold temperatures seemed to have any effect on its people. You looked at Haji's concerned gaze, knowing he was worrying that you would lose your temper and tell them what you had been doing that afternoon. But he needed not worry - you would not be so reckless. But you would not sit by either, when your friends were being so blatantly deceived, 'Everything they tell us in those doctrines serves to make us believe that Darm is the only civilization on Artica,' you said. 'How can you accept their word without searching for proof?'

Sitting between you and Sophie, Haji quietly listened to your argument, realizing that he would soon have to pick sides between the two darmians he cared for the most.

'We are given have all the proof we need,' Sophie intervened, staring at you harshly. 'And I think the only reason you are so suspicious about the Council of Mentalists is because you blame them for not having two caretakers. And you spend so much time alone in your residence that you feel the need to go out and break Directives just so you feel better. But the worst part is that you take Haji with you,' she added callously.

You turned your eyes to the soothing sea and fell into a brooding silence. Sophie had spoken her heart much out of concern for the well being of Haji, you knew, but you could not help but feel that she was right. An overwhelming sadness filled your mind and even though you were surrounded by your friends, you felt alone.

Realizing she had said more than she needed to prove her point, Sophie broke the silence, 'Alan, my most sincere apology. I did not mean to say that,' she said, her voice sounding as remorseful as the look in her eyes.

You allowed a sad smile to brighten your face, 'It's okay Sophie. I know you worry for Haji's sake,' you said, and a feeling of joy washed away your sadness when you remembered a comforting fact, 'besides, I don't live alone. I have Evander and Hampy to keep me company.'

Jack looked sideways at Cathy, 'An overzealous host and an outdated droid are hardly any company,' he murmured audibly and snickered.

Cathy stomped his foot painfully, 'It is a lot better than having you as a friend!'

You started feeling embarrassed and wanted to move away from the spotlight that had fallen upon you, 'But you're right Sophie, when you say I shouldn't involve Haji.'

Haji widened his eyes at you, realizing the moment had come.

'However,' you added, grinning at him wickedly. 'I do think he is entitled to an opinion.'

Haji was flanked by your stares, as you and Sophie waited for his answer. He shrank into the seat, hoping the conversation would fade into thoughtless remarks.

'You are right Alan,' said Sophie, a shrewd look in her eyes. 'What is your opinion, Haji?'

Without any chance to escape, Haji wished he could crawl under the seat and disappear. He did not want to pick sides, for he knew that if he did, his action would reinforce one relationship at the detriment of the other. So he glanced around, saw the restless look in Cathy's face, and hastily crafted a solution that would allow him to dodge the question - assuming Cathy would intervene as he expected her to.

'Well...in my opinion... – *your eyes widened* - I think Acolytes will do just fine.'

'Precisely!' Cathy stepped in, throwing a finger in the air. 'Thank you Haji!'

Cathy's intervention proved Haji's assumption right. He sighed with relief as Sophie snarled at him and looked away.

'I am glad I finally had an opportunity to step in,' Cathy added. 'This discussion was making me really uncomfortable. You two should know best not to have that kind of conversation. That is a serious attempt against Darm's order.'

'My apology Cathy. You are absolutely correct,' Sophie answered.

''We have completely diverted from our intended subject and needlessly allowed ourselves to hurt one another. Alan?' Cathy called.

You were distracted, listening to the sound of the sea and thinking about what Sophie had said. Coming out of the slumber, you gave her a weary absent look, 'My apology. Go on.'

'Let's continue planning the Gathering,' she added.

'Let's do it!' said Jack, slapping his hands on the table and bouncing on the seat, catching everyone by surprise. 'We have a Gathering to prepare. And it is going to be *googoltastically* awesome!'

Cathy had previously arranged a list of tasks she intended to divide amongst her friends in accordance with the knowledge each possessed. She took her *neuropad* from her utility belt and unrolled it on the table.

'Alan and Haji, I need you to generate the Coating Device's codes of the props that will be decorating the suite and the costumes we will be wearing,' she said.

You nodded and turned your attention to the blue sea. Haji however, in his eagerness for solving every complex situation he was confronted with, quickly began drawing a mental sketch of the source codes required to build the props and costumes.

'Jacky have you spoken to your caretaker about the appetizers?' Cathy asked next.

Jack stretched his arm around her and released his huge glinting smile, 'Yes my prized pyrea. The appetizers are being created in the Second Quadrant Manufacturing Facility, where they will be stored and await the day they shall merrily journey into your good looking mouth.'

She pulled his arm away, 'Charming.' Then she turned her attention to Sophie, 'In that case all that remains is our part: choosing the theme.'

'I think Tropical is the best choice,' Sophie risked the suggestion, pouting her lips.

'Oh no! No more Tropical!' said Cathy.

'But it's so pleasant, so warm and so full of light! It's how the Island of Retirement must look like,' she turned her eyes to the tranquil beach behind Cathy and Jack.

'You will have plenty of time to stay on the island after you fulfil your goals as a citizen. Retirement is still one too many years away,' said Cathy. 'I was thinking of a more intriguing theme: the animals from the Age of the Antiga Pyre. I've been to the Historic

Records[21] this afternoon and I browsed through some of the exemplars. They were fascinating,' she added, her amber eyes staring blankly at the blue sky, 'quite fascinating.'

You and your friends shared a dull stare.

As Cathy and Sophie chattered between themselves about which theme was the best, you had a calm conversation with Haji and Jack. Twice Jack interrupted their conversation to offer an uninformed opinion, mostly suggestions of sleazy costumes for girls.

'Why do you strain yourselves choosing a theme?' he said slyly after they dismissed his suggestions countless times. 'Simple and light garments would do just fine and are far less cumbersome. Why must you put so much thought into it?'

They utterly ignored him.

Sophie's initial disappointment regarding Cathy's choice had turned into pleased expectations as Cathy explained to her some of her ideas for the costumes. After a tiresome hour they had finally decided on the theme. Then, they moved on to the selection of the props for the suite, and as their uninteresting chatter prolonged, you and Haji ran out of topics of conversation. You started to insist on leaving, lightly elbowing Haji, who in turn elbowed you back. Jack was snoring already, his head lying on the back of the seat and a thin line of saliva dripping down the red coating from his partly opened mouth. Cathy and Sophie were still wearily yet merrily discussing the theme when Colt announced, with the precision of a clock, that the time had come to close the establishment. You thanked the moment when all of you left the Retreat, drowsy and nodding, and took your steps upon the snow-laden Coastal Walkway, whose path faded into the night. Beyond, was the vast darkness of the sea, whose frozen waters already slept quietly.

Cathy and Jack bid their leave and climbed onto a platform, catching the Panoramic Way to the tall skyscrapers of the Specialist Class Sector. You and your remaining friends followed down the East Boulevard until entering one of the main roads of the Administrator Class Sector. After bowing, you turned to your street and pursued your path towards a good night's rest. Haji and Sophie lived on the same block. Therefore, they trudged down their street together, chatting and giggling.

Each block was composed of an agglomerate of adjunct residences. They were identical in every aspect, something that usually befuddled you when returning to your residence at night. Was it not for your own personalized front entrance and you would have skipped it when you were walking past it. Even with the dim light coming from the street lamps, you managed to perceive an untended patio that had disappeared under a meter of snow along with its chairs and table. You pushed the knee-height gate aside and stepped inside, dragging your legs through the snow. Beneath your narrow porch you glanced at the tidy terrace from the adjacent residence, the Sylvere's residence, and grimaced.

You looked at the silvery lunoids above, 'I hope Miriam can't see this from above,' you whispered, sighed and entered.

The day had ended, and so you lied in bed and slept. And in due time I might add, for Sleep Time had fallen upon Darm and every darmian was required to rest. So rest you did, unaware that you had woven one more thread into the fabric of destiny that would lead you to where you stand now. I cannot help but wonder. If you had known the consequences, would you have still fallen asleep during that History indoctrination? Or answered mentor Levine the way you did?

...I do not regret my actions...

Indeed you do not, for now…

Fifth memory – Anatomy of a virus

[...] and the economy shall be based on the awarding and removal of Credits, the sole currency of the metropolis. The Artificial Intelligence shall continuously monitor the performance of every darmian, from their early stage as an infant up to their final stage as a citizen, and regardless of the stage, the better a darmian will be at performing his tasks, the greater the Credits she shall award them with. As a result of this economic system, the Artificial Intelligence shall be able to maintain a stable balance between the requirements and aptitudes of its inhabitants, ensure equal opportunities to each and every one of them, and instil in them from an early age a reward-based mentality that shall greatly enhance productivity.

An excerpt from Annex #03: Currency and Reward Directives; Division of Darmian Affairs under the authority of Mentalist Silas;

The next week flew by as the expectations regarding citizenship grew. The turn to citizenship was a decisive event for all darmians, for it was the moment they were required to choose the occupation they would perform for the rest of their existence. Therefore, along with your growing expectation grew an even greater dread, for you had not yet decided on an occupation that would award your existence with a sense of accomplishment. You hoped however, that when the time came, you would make the right choice, and the finalists Gathering was just the right occasion to find some inspiration, as it represented your last opportunity for entertainment, and maybe one of the last moments you had to enjoy your time with many of your colleagues. As the week stretched on, one day was left before the day of the Gathering.

That morning, the metropolis was aroused by the sound of the usual host of citizens flowing in the streets and Boulevards, on their way to their occupations like orderly rivers coursing through ridges of permaglass. Most of them were on foot and all were distinguishable by the colour of their uniforms: green for apprentices, yellow for Manufacturing and Spaceport administrators, violet for Hub administrators and mentors, and white for the elite citizens, the Project Specialists. These wore stern faces, their tall slender bodies clad in white filing over the white marbled pavement as an embodiment of the metropolis herself.

As you strolled down the colourful East Boulevard, you felt the presence of your Unit as she warned you of a communications request from Haji. You conveyed the thought to accept it, and you felt your mind expand beyond your thoughts.

'If you do not slow down we will not be able to catch up with you,' Haji's faceless voice echoed in your mind.

'Where are you?' you thought as if you were speaking to him.

'Look behind you,' his voice answered.

You looked back and saw ten meters away Haji and Sophie dressed in their green uniforms, walking through the myriad of colours. You stopped and waited for them, making use of the respite to take the last bite on the nutrient bar, which was becoming as cold and tasteless as snow.

'Salutations Haji,' you greeted each one with a bow. 'Salutations Sophie.'

Since the day Haji revealed his affection for her in the Academy hallway - however indirect as it might have been - he and Sophie had become close companions. At times they would exchange smiles and laughter, and even an occasional hug whenever they were out of sight of sentinels and of the draconian scrutiny of Council representatives, for any gesture of intimacy was deemed as unnecessary body contact as was considered a breach of the Directives for Proper Conduct.

'Salutations Alan,' Sophie cordially replied. 'Ready for a new day of indoctrination?'

You nodded, demonstrating an odd enthusiasm for the perspective, 'As ready as I can be.'

As you strode on, walking behind a straight line of mentors and apprentices entering the Academy, you whispered to Haji with a sidelong glance, 'The Gathering is tomorrow.'

'I know,' he answered smiling.

Walking past the two dark-blue sentinels guarding its western entrance, you entered the vast white plaza. Before you was a majestic curved building with its inner facade facing the Netcore. Like all buildings in Darm, its surface was covered in permaglass, save for the tall frame that sustained it, which was made of glinting *impermium*[22].

Climbing its wide stairway and crossing the wide open doors, you followed the two orderly rows of apprentices entering the building. Although you were many, you did not hear a sound when you entered the hallway, save for the sound of footsteps on its pristine marble floor.

The indoctrination rooms were aligned throughout the inner arch of the hallway with their corresponding number marked above their entrance. When you entered the *"#465"* indoctrination room, you saw the mentor of Fundaments of Existence standing on the dais in front of her apprentices while waiting patiently for the signal to begin indoctrination; sitting at their desks some apprentices exchanged quiet conversations. When a clear sharp note echoed through the corridors and into the indoctrination room, the sliding door behind sealed shut and the apprentices' murmurs faded into an absolute silence. The mentor smiled and approached the first row of desks, bowing afterwards.

'Salutations apprentices. Today we shall begin our final theme before your rightful admittance to citizenship. Once we have completed it, you shall have an extensive understanding of the pathogen that forever changed Pyre's genetic code.'

To most of the apprentices, the mentor had an unremarkable voice, but to your ears, her voice was kind and enthralling, much unlike the dull scratchy voice of mentor Levine.

'Who amongst you can share some knowledge about the retrovirus that put an end to the Antiga Pyre?' she asked.

A few hands rose above the silent audience, belonging to apprentices that placidly waited being called on to answer. Amongst them was Sophie's, and her eyes glinted as she restrained her excitement.

'Very well, we have four apprentices who have prepared this indoctrination. Those of you who have raised your hand shall give a chained answer. Apprentice Lauren, do you care to begin?' she asked turning her attention to Heidi.

Heidi lowered her hand and sat straight in her second-row desk, placing one hand on top of the other, and answered with her sharp voice:

'The entity known as PIn-T2, was a non-lethal retrovirus whose transmission to the host was achieved through any liquid medium. It could be absorbed through the respiratory system by means of airborne aerosols released from a contaminated host, digestive system by means of ingestion of contaminated water or food containing water, or its most effective mean, the transmission of fluids though body contact which led to direct absorption by the circulatory system.

'Very well,' interrupted the mentor. 'Apprentice Adams you may continue,' she said pointing to Andrew, an apprentice with whom you were not very well acquainted even though he always bore a friendly expression.

Andrew spoke with proud confidence, which by itself demonstrated his desire of completing his apprenticeship as one of the top ranked apprentices:

'The retrovirus belonged to the Oxygen-Nitrogen based macromolecules, containing in itself a reactive strand of nucleotides. Its organic structure was highly unstable due to the presence of ionized phosphate groups on its skeleton, which in conjunction with its sedimentation velocity allowed it to adhere with great ease to the eukaryotic cells of the Pyre. Once it reached the circulatory system, the retrovirus penetrated the cells by attaching itself to the nucleotides of the genetic code.'

'Well done apprentice Adams,' the mentor encouraged.

Andrew gave her a proud look while the mentor directed her attention to Sophie, 'Apprentice Andersen you may continue.'

'The adherence process of the viral RNA strand to the DNA molecules of the host's cells took place in the *S-phase*, where simply put, a cell's DNA molecules split into two and form two other DNA molecules. The adherence of the viral strand was made possible due to the enzyme *integrase* that allowed the retrovirus to become part of a cell's DNA through a *reverse transcriptase* process. As a result, when the S-phase was completed the cell entered the *mitosis* phase and formed two new cells carrying the viral DNA strand. These infected cells would then carry on replicating more infected cells through the regular cell cycle. For this reason, the enzyme *integrase* was one of the fundamental components of the retrovirus, as it served as the tool that allowed it to become part of the cell's genetic code and establish a lifelong infection in the host.'

Haji nodded at her and his lips moved, saying *"Superb"*. She smiled back.

'Well presented, apprentice Andersen,' and the mentor bowed to her. 'Apprentice Emerson you may conclude.'

Francis sank down on his chair and answered timidly:

'I have not attained much more knowledge of the subject, mentor Elias. From what I learned by researching the Database, what I know is after a new host had been infected, its cells reproduced the retrovirus macromolecule which in turn would release itself into the environment and find new hosts through liquid medium, as Heidi mentioned.'

'Thus completing the cycle,' mentor Elias added. Her green eyes glinted with satisfaction and her slender face was filled with a gentle smile. 'Well done. I am proud of my apprentices.'

...she was kind...and beautiful...

She was. It was since your earliest days as an apprentice that you nurtured an uncommon admiration for her. To you, every aspect of her was pleasant and proportional. Her white teeth aligned perfectly behind her thin red lips, her amber eyes warmed your heart every time she looked upon you; her captivating smile carried your thoughts away to bold fantasies. Her firm bosoms filled her tight violet uniform, her waist was as smooth as a wave function, her fertile hips and her lean thighs urged you to ---

...leave my fantasies out of this and get on with this meaningless subject...

Forgive me. I shall resume. However, this subject was not as meaningless as you might consider. Within it was an understanding to the retrovirus which no one except Gadim was able to fully grasp. He saw the genetic code as it truly was, and he realized how it flawed the Pyre, turning your kind into something that I never intended it to be.

The mentor turned to the window-wall and interacted with it, using the *neurolink*[23] that rested comfortably on her right ear. The view of the Academy's inner plaza was replaced by an opaque screen of information relating to the subject of Fundaments of

Existence, whose seemingly endless topics filled the wall from top to bottom. Using Thought Interaction, she accessed the topic *"PIn-S2"* and then the sub-topic *"Epidemiology"*.

On the screen were displayed several images demonstrating a sequence of the infection process of the retrovirus. In one of the images, the macromolecule seemed to be in interaction with an isolated *eukaryotic* cell; in another was plainly visible the strand of nucleotides that Heidi had described. The images seemed to be divided in four stages and the mentor began to explain the first stage, mentioning with approval the common points that her apprentices had presented. Arriving at the second stage, she sat behind her desk and continued:

'On the second stage of incubation, we can see that the affected cells of the organism now comprise over seventy percent of the cell population, with a prevalence of approximately thirty percent on the bone tissue. In this stage, the group of signs and symptoms were still inexistent or unspecific. As a consequence, it was still not possible to ascertain without clinical trial whether an organism was infected or not.'

Her soft voice was so alluring that you followed her every move and every word, from her calm gestures pointing towards the three-dimensional images, to her occasional pauses to assess whether she could continue or whether she had to explain once more.

'On entering the third stage,' she continued, 'the incubation had successfully reached the point of irreversibility, and any attempt to eradicate the retrovirus resulted in the destruction of its host. This irreversibility is one of the two reasons why this pathogen was so effective at spreading throughout the globalized societies of the antigans. The other reason was that the host was already infectious during the incubation process, meaning that the retrovirus was free to replicate itself and spread to new hosts without any signs of infection being displayed by the carrier.'

After mentor Elias highlighted the last stage of the incubation process, the screen reproduced an animation of the retrovirus neutralizing the cell's defences and attaching itself to a DNA strand. Its effectiveness was both admirable and shocking.

She pointed one finger to a segment of the altered DNA, 'Once fully lodged inside the still asymptomatic host, the viral RNA strand migrated from the cells' nucleus to the cells' mitochondria, lodging themselves in the DNA of this structure. The incision of the vRNA in the cell mitochondria caused a chain mutation of mitochondrial DNA, creating a pattern with a specific codon sequence known to be the Torment trigger sequence. The mitochondria's more resistant RNA molecules were unable as well to prevent this mutation due to the hypersecretion of oxygen reactive composites by the retrovirus, which neutralized their attempts to repair the damaged DNA strands. When the fourth stage was complete, the mitochondrial DNA became viral and the said sequence triggered the start of the chain mutation,' said the mentor, pointing to the schematics where the viral RNA performed an alteration of the mitochondrial DNA. 'The first of our Guiding Father's accomplishments was to discover that the transition from the incubation phase to the Torment phase followed a chain recoding of the DNA that would only commence once the mitochondria population of the host was entirely contaminated, which means that the Torment phase would wait until the incubation phase had been completed,' she said and waited for the apprentices to finish their annotations. 'There are no accurate predictions of the time span of the incubation phase, but simulations run by Mother suggest that this process lasted for twenty to thirty years, and we now know that this viral RNA was also able to infect the host's gametes during *meiosis*. This was one of our Guiding Father's most important discoveries as it allowed us to entirely understand the cause of the extinction of the Antiga Pyre. It is believed, that once an offspring from an infected antigan attempted to breed with a non infected antigan, the result would be an infertile hybrid. This means that throughout the Age of Obscurity, as all the surviving populations became infected, the Antiga Pyre withered away and eventually became extinct.'

She granted the apprentices some time to convey into their neuropads what she had said. Then, she added, answering to some keen eyes, 'This is one of the reasons why all darmians are fertilized and bred in controlled laboratory conditions and then appointed to caretakers. However, it is still a futile effort to reverse our offspring's genetic code to that of our ancestors. It may even prove impossible, since the original code was lost when the antigans became extinct.'

You raised your hand, as much out of curiosity as to grab her attention, 'Why were the antigans unable to remove the genetic flaw from their gene pool?'

'That is a good question apprentice Balthazar,' she answered as you welcomed her tender gaze. 'The reason is that the retrovirus did not perform a linear mutation of the Antiga Pyre's DNA. Instead, it unevenly spread throughout their genetic code in small and very discrete codon sequences, some of them redundant, others self-reconstructive, and others seemingly normal, yet all interlinked through a recently discovered process.'

'That was one smart germ!' Jack allowed himself to shout.

The class erupted in a half-suppressed laughter.

Mentor Elias calmly gazed at him, 'It was indeed apprentice Thompson, and that is why it was successful in leading an entire species to self-extinction. You should have some respect for it, and for our ancestors.'

One by one, the apprentices quieted down, gazing at the mentor in solemn contemplation.

'My apology, mentor Elias. I did not mean to disrespect them,' Jack spoke embarrassedly to the silent room.

'Apology accepted,' she said, throwing him a courteous smile.

After a brief pause, the mentor moved on to the next topic: *"Pathophysiology."*

The lights in the room waned and she continued the indoctrination on the holoprojector, letting the morning light into the room through the shaded window-wall:

'We shall now address the symptoms that the Nova Pyre has come to refer to as the Torment. These symptoms, or *manifestations,* are the reason why from antigan civilization there are only buried remnants, broken artifacts, and weather-beaten ruins.'

Hovering above the holoprojector emerged a physical representation of an antigan, slowly rotating along a vertical axis. Its body was stubby and hairy, its skin soft and pinkish, its face beardy and brutish.

...they were not much different from pyreans...

Evolution from Antiga Pyre to Nova Pyre had effected mild changes to the Pyre's constitution. Some of the changes were discrete, such as the loss of all hair in the body, apart from the head, eyebrows and eyelashes. Other were more noticeable: they became taller and slenderer, and their countenance uncommonly fairer and more delicate, changes that occurred because attractiveness became the sole criterion of natural selection between pyreans during the Age of Obscurity.

'The Torment can be divided into two sets of symptoms,' said mentor Elias. 'The *Localized Morphological Manifestations* and the *Widespread Morphological Manifestations,* which, as the name suggests, are either localized or widespread alterations in our body appearance. These can be temporary, or in more severe cases permanent, and are a result of the change in the genetic code responsible for our appearance.'

Mentor Elias continued to explain the Torment, using the antigan model to demonstrate different manifestations. Your astonishment grew increasingly as the model assumed various grotesque forms. On one of the *Localized Manifestations,* the model suffered shocking alterations to the arms; these increased in size, changing shape and radically changing their texture and colour to a rugged and reddish glow.

She then moved on to the *Widespread Morphological Manifestations,* your astonishment turned into disbelief. On one of the first manifestations, the model grew to almost three times its size and his skin turned into a ridged shell with a brownish hue; his already brutish face became heinously deformed, the lips thick and dark, the eyes deeply burrowed into the skull as if they had been sucked in by some incomprehensible force, and his hair had extended down to its body and thickened to become a layer of menacingly sharp thorns. On one of the last manifestations the model became utterly repulsive, its skin turning into a sickening green paste, and becoming so languid it seemed to melt off of its body; its limbs were reduced to large tentacles, and on its edges grew blotches and pustules, some of them erupting with a yellow slimy fluid. No apprentice was unmoved by the manifestation. Many ended up averting their eyes, and Marlene, an apprentice with a peculiarly pale skin-tone, which had become white as marble at that point, ended up throwing up her breakfast on the floor. It was after that incident that mentor Elias decided to stop the demonstrations and interrupted the indoctrination, allowing the apprentices to recover and share their thoughts while she accompanied Marlene to the wash room.

You took the time to talk to Haji, stealing his attention from his neuropad, 'What do you think of this?' you asked feeling both curious and suspicious.

Haji gave you an upset look, 'It troubles me to know that we have the Torment inside us. Without the Personal Identification Unit we would be vulnerable to it. Our Guiding Father might not be as great has He claims to be, but we still have to thank Him for what He has accomplished. He helped the Pyre reclaim its place in Artica and allowed its societies to rebuild once more.

You looked at your neuropad as the image of the manifestation rotated inside it, 'Maybe you're right…' you yielded while withholding some doubt.

...what a grand deception...

A little while after, mentor Elias returned with Marlene at her side. The apprentice was grasping her stomach but her skin was a little less pale, which led you to assume she was feeling a little better. After dragging her feet back to her desk, she sat, quite, slowly. The mentor returned to her place alongside the holoprojector and waited until the apprentices returned to their silent awareness before proceeding:

'I would like to end this indoctrination with a quick note. As you are aware, any change that occurs on a given system, however erratic it may seem, has to obey to a specific set of Laws. It is only because of Laws that we are able to predict the motion of the stars and galaxies, the weather patterns that determine Artica's climate, the cycle of our existence, and yes, even the Torment,' she said and became quiet, seeming intended to incite curiosity. After sitting behind her desk and quietly conveying some thoughts to her neuropad she continued, 'As such, I wish you to research the set of Laws related to the Torment as they are presented in Gadim's Theorem regarding Phenotype Rearrangement which shall be the theme for the upcoming indoctrination. The criteria for Credits awarded shall be adequate exposure of the topic, comprehensibility of the presented topic and conclusions drawn from the research. The respective Credits are five, ten and fifteen.' She rose from her seat and walked towards the edge of the dais, 'Does anyone wish for me to clarify any subject?'

A torrent of arms were raised, yet given the short amount of time before the signal, mentor Elias allowed only one question. To be impartial in her choice, she used her neurolink to generate a random name and then present it on the walls so that everyone could see. Leonard was the apprentice Mother chose, highlighting his name in big letters on the walls.

Leonard was not the type of apprentice that would actively participate in any discussion. Throughout the years he had developed – nearly at a mastery level - the ability to pay attention to both the indoctrinations and Heidi, an apprentice he had become irresistibly infatuated with. During any given indoctrination he would devote his ears to the mentor, and his eyes to Heidi, who was sitting next to him. When he saw his name floating on the walls he felt his ruse had been discovered, and Heidi's eyes and hears had now turned to him. He could not help but feel that somehow he was being punished, since now he had no other choice but to become the centre of her attention.

He asked with a tremulous shrill voice, 'Mentor Elias, I understood how the retrovirus managed to spread throughout the Antiga Pyre and create us. And I also understood what manifestations are. But what I did not understand – *he glanced at*

Heidi before continuing – or at least not too well, is why the Torment has so many different manifestations.'

Mentor Elias' delighted gaze gave Leonard confidence and he smiled with satisfaction. She was delighted with the apropos question. It had been the first time Leonard had participated in her indoctrinations and yet he had managed to identify the mystery behind the Torment.

'That is an excellent question apprentice Leonard. No doubt some of you are unable to understand the reason as to the enormous diversity of manifestations - *some apprentices nodded their heads.* – Unfortunately, the reason can only be revealed to those who succeed in becoming Project Specialists.'

His satisfaction waned into an expression of disappointment. Conversely, a look satisfaction grew in some faces - Heidi's included - for they knew they would surely achieve Specialist Class.

'However!' mentor Elias added, pouting her lips slyly, 'one could speculate – *her eyes probed the ceiling* – that there could be a correlation between these manifestations and the way we experience emotions.'

Bewilderment is the most appropriate word to describe the look on the apprentice's faces, yours included. Most did not make any sense of her words; some found it so surprising that they raised their hands to ask for a more comprehensive explanation.

'I would be delighted to engage in further speculation,' mentor Elias continued, 'regretfully, this more confusing than explanatory hypothesis will have to suffice.'

The indoctrination ended a few seconds later, leaving the room full of disappointed apprentices. One by one, they rolled up their *neuropads* and packed them in their utility belts, leaving the room orderly while engaged in quiet arguments. Mentor Elias remained at her desk, conveying thoughts to her neurolink. Heidi approached the desk and attempted – yet unsuccessfully - to ask for an explanation. As vain as the attempt might have been, for Leonard it was the appropriate excuse to walk up to her side and start a conversation. And so he did, shyly.

Sixth memory – Tales of the long departed

[...] leading me to the conclusion that instinct and emotion became the never-ending source for all the tragedy that befell the Antiga Pyre. Further experimental research performed on infants nurtured in simulated wildlife environments revealed behaviours that in some cases surpassed even the savagery of animals, whereas the control group, when deprived from any other contact with nature, had their instincts and emotions rendered latent. This outcome could be explained by the biological affinity that we have to these animals, namely the mammals. Despite the fact that not all fauna and flora were extinct during the Age of Obscurity, it is highly recommended that darmians be kept isolated from the surviving species and the only information available regarding this matter be related to the extinct species that once co-existed with us. Furthermore, they should be known to darmians only as animals and each should be named by their scientific nomenclature, a contingency that shall uphold a sense of singularity of the pyrean species and possibly instil in them a sense of alienation that will extinguish any affinities for animals that may arise. Regardless of the outcome, I recommend continuing the research in the field of genetic remapping, and attempt to remove instinct and emotion and every other genetic fault from the Pyre gene pool altogether. Although most of the first

experiments were unsuccessful, some failed specimen revealed significant improvements.

An excerpt from Annex #9: On biological seclusion; Division of Darmian Affairs under the authority of Mentalist Silas;

With *Lunch Time* upon Darm, the vast mess hall of the tenth floor of the Academy was immersed in racket, warmth and flavours. The large curved window-wall opposite the entrance allowed Mithras to shine its light upon the multitude of green uniforms. Apprentices sat and stood, chatted and chewed, pointed forks at each other and scraped the remainders of food from their dishes. Their lunches were being handed to them through a long line of *food generators*[24] on top of metallic counters, which were located on the edges of the curved hall.

After ordering and collecting the food trays, your group sat side-by-side and face-to-face at the only table in the mess hall: an enormous curved table that extended from one edge of the hall to the other. Resting on the table in front of you, on a round metal plate, was your meal as you ordered it: a blue carbohydrates jelly cube, a colourful emulsion of mineral, a triangular prism of fibres, and a sliced brown cylinder of proteins; on a cup next to your plate was your favourite drink, a sweet and sour vitamin shake. Altogether, they comprised a third of your R.D.D., as was determined by your Unit's vital statistics.

While everyone enjoyed their meal, Cathy grabbed the opportunity to learn about the preparations for the Gathering:

'How are the codes for the Coating Device coming along?' she asked you and Haji, with a hint of concern.

'They are practically written,' Haji answered, sitting at your side. 'All there is left to do is re-check the coding lines, which I will be doing this evening. I believe you are going to find the makeovers quite appealing, but you really must congratulate Alan for the designs. He wrote the lines for the animal costumes by himself.'

Cathy smiled at you from across the table, her eyes glittering with satisfaction, 'Excellent!' Cathy applauded. 'The preparations are coming along as we expected.'

'It is excellent indeed!' said Sophie, sitting next to Cathy. 'I came to worry that we were going to have to postpone the Gathering due to mentor Levine's bonus presentation. We might owe everything to your efforts Alan.'

Instead of doing research for the presentation you found that working on the codes was the best way to spend your Rest Time. Now, you felt comforted in knowing that you had helped all finalists, and you saw it as an amends for all the troubles you had caused to many of them due to your several misguided conducts throughout apprenticeship.

'It was my pleasure,' you answered with a distracted smile, your thoughts more focused on your food.

'Moving on,' said Cathy, 'it was the unanimous decision of all finalists that each of us will select one animal and present it on our Individual Presentation. The selection will be done according to the Standings – *you hung your head disappointedly* – *but!* the organizers take priority over everyone else.'

'I've already chosen mine,' you promptly announced.

'I have already chosen mine as well,' Haji added.

Sophie and Cathy stared with surprise at each other.

'And which was your choice?' Sophie asked, a look of curiosity on her face.

Your words came out in a blend of simplicity and reverence, revealing your admiration for the animal, '*Ailuropoda melanoleuca.*'

Jack gave you a dumbfounded stare, 'What is that?'

'*Ailuropoda melanoleuca* is the designation given to a peculiar animal. Traces of its existence were found on the oriental borders of the East Continent,' explained Cathy.

'And what makes it so peculiar?' asked Jack.

'Well, besides having a furry and adorable look, it is believed that though it shared an affinity with predators, it fed exclusively on a unique vegetable and was very affable,' said Cathy. Then she teased you, 'Did you pick him because he reflects your personality?'

You flushed and took a spoonful of fibres to your mouth just so you did not have to answer.

Sophie's curiosity was not yet sated, so she took the opportunity to ask, 'What about you Haji, which one did you pick?'

Haji gave her a simple yet proud smile, 'Of the few costumes that I managed to encode, the one I found most alluring was the *Linx pardinus*. I was astonished by its spots and long ruffs of fur beneath the chin. They were magnificent animals.'

Sophie's lips drew a soft captivating smile, 'That is interesting. I have considered choosing one that bears a strong resemblance to the *Lynx pardinus.*'

'You have?' he asked, and now it was his turn to feel curious, 'Which one is it?'

She nodded her head and hid her lips inside her mouth to arrest her desire to tell. Instead she answered with a infantile infatuation, '*Nuh uh*...I cannot say. It will be a surprise.'

'That is not fair! I told you mine,' complained Haji. Oddly to him, when gazing at her bright brown eyes the disconnected word "*jubatus*" came to his thoughts. He ignored the word entirely as he did not see her lips move.

Sophie flicked her auburn hair at him and smiled in sweet defiance, 'I did not make you,' she answered with a delighted tone and winked at him across the table. 'Trust me, *my favourite darmian*. It will be a lot more interesting when you find out.'

Haji smiled and forgot about the entire subject admiring her attractive smile, and when a strange and out-of-place silence sunk in, he realized that the rest of their friends were staring at them with amused, astonished and happy faces.

'Where did that come from?' asked an astonished Jack.

'It does not concern you,' Cathy answered with an amused smile. 'Now moving on. Which attires shall the rest of us choose?'

'I want a fierce animal!' Jack jumped in as loud as he could. 'The fiercest of them all!'

'In that case choose the *Panthera leo*,' suggested Cathy, remembering her awe when she saw its animation in the Historical Records. 'It is considered by our Specialists to be the fiercest and most terrifying animal that existed in the obscure age. He had a formidable mane that encompassed his entire head and chest.'

'That one! That's the one!' said Jack raising his finger to the air and unleashing his disproportionate smile.

You spoke between a feigned coughing and a sidelong glance to Haji, 'I don't know if the mane can compete with his humongous smile.

Everyone laughed except for Jack. He frowned at you while you looked up at the metallic ceiling, your hands behind your head.

'Mock me all you want,' retorted Jack in his self-assured wittiness, 'but when the Gathering starts and you ask me to introduce you to some of my female acquaintances you'll see how *humendous* my smile can be.'

You leaned forward and gave him a humble smile, 'Come on Jacky, I'm just complimenting your smile. I was saying that nothing can compete with it.'

Jack was pleased with your excuse, and his face changed from disgruntled to smiley, 'Nothing can indeed. And since I am in such good mood, you can count on me to present you to some of the apprentices from class "#477". Some of them have been asking me questions about you, ever since they learned of your daring response to mentor Levine.'

Cathy's amused smile waned and she lowered her eyes to her tray. You managed to notice, and an unsettling sense of helplessness urged you to speak to her. But you did not know how.

'Well the Gathering's purpose is to allow finalists to find the right companion. I am sure you will find one for you Alan,' she said glancing at you with disappointment.

A veil of silence fell on you corner of the vast table, surrounded by the echoes of clattering and racketing of cutlery and dishes and trays.

'I can hardly believe we have only four more weeks before completing the tenth and last year of apprenticeship,' groaned Jack with his mouth full. 'After that, it is time for a residence of my own and some quality time with my companion.'

Sophie gave him an absent nod.

'It is not long now until we become citizens,' said Cathy.

'Not long now,' you muttered, staring outside the window, your mind besieged by great unease.

...I dreaded that moment...

'What do you think mentor Elias meant by suggesting that the Torment is related to the way we experience emotions?' you suddenly asked, curious about her words and wanting to change topic. 'There was something in the way she spoke, a hidden intention.'

'It was just a hypothesis Alan,' said Sophie.

'A curious one indeed,' added Haji. 'That manifestations may be somehow related to emotions is a disturbing prospect.'

Jack picked up pieces of jelly from his plate, placed two pointy pieces between his teeth and lips and two other round pieces on his eyes, 'Look at me, I'm angry and I'm becoming a pestilent creature! *Booh! Boooh!'* he said, raising claw-shaped hands at Cathy.

'That you are,' she retorted indifferently.

The pieces fell from his face and he added with displeasure, 'Come on! Are we seriously going to change topics only to feed Alan's hunger for whatever is that he likes to feed on? Theories about how the indoctrinations are meant to deceive us and the sort...'

You smiled at him. For once you agreed with him, 'You're right Jack, the Gathering is tomorrow and we have better things to talk about.'

'And I can barely wait any longer!' Cathy added, rousing the mood. 'I want to see how I look in my animal costume. The virtual illustration did not leave me too impressed. I might have to add some adornments,' she added with a sly look on her face.

As she curled her red hair around a finger she occasionally cast her amber eyes at you, neither smiling nor frowning. You smiled at her absentmindedly.

'I still cannot understand. Why all that interest for a costume?' Jack asked while he filled the fork.

'I do not expect you to understand,' Cathy answered, her eyes looking at the empty tray, her head resting on one hand.

Jack shrugged and filled his mouth with food.

'That's because there is nothing to understand,' he concluded while chewing. 'You girls make a fuss out of everything.'

'Jack, the Gathering is the official occasion for a finalist to choose a *companion*[25],' Haji explained. 'It is a very important moment for us as our choice will determine whom we will be spending the rest of our existence with.'

Sophie looked at him coyly, 'What about you Haji, is it a very important moment for you?' Sophie asked him, hiding her face behind her auburn hair.

Haji looked at her and when her bright brown eyes met his hazel eyes he answered softly, 'I have already chosen my companion.'

Sophie's eyes shone bright as morning stars and she smiled with absolute delight. Even you, who were still worrying about becoming a citizen were drawn to that moment. It was such an important decision for your best friend that you felt an immense joy for him and for Sophie.

Cathy was happy for her as well and she smiled at them, suppressing a natural hint of envy.

'Well if no one wants you I can throw in a favour Cathy,' said a completely oblivious Jack with his mouthful.

If eyes could melt, Cathy's stare would have disintegrated Jack.

'Jacky!' Sophie intervened in a cheerful yelp, still overjoyed by Haji's indirect proposal.

Jack realized everyone was staring at him.

'What?!' he shrugged, 'I am just saying, if Cathy can't find anyone I don't mind being her companion.'

Cathy leaned over the table and answered, smoothly, 'Jacky, I rather have the pestilent creature that made Marlene throw up.'

The table was filled with warm laughter.

'Ouch Cathy, that's harsh,' he answered, apparently unscathed.

'That's well deserved!' you added while laughing.

Throughout the rest of *Lunch Time* many apprentices enjoyed the fresh air outside, strolling on the grey granite slabs of the courtyard surrounding the Academy's massive building. The courtyard was decorated with elegant imposing sculptures made of polished gray stone, depicting some of the most memorable mentors to ever exist. Tall and sparkling water fountains mixed with antifreeze and long benches which were kept warm and dry by an imbued heating device were scattered about. You and Cathy sat on one of them and enjoyed a truly admirable view of the Netcore. Like a tall pillar of light she rose from the Central Circle and pierced the clear blue sky, reflecting Mithras as it shone upon her permaglass and impermium countenance. Jack was standing next to you, but he was distracted from the conversation you were having with Cathy, being rather engaged in the repetitive task of greeting female apprentices with his large disproportionate smile as they walked by. Sophie and Haji were keeping a private distance from the rest of the group. Sometimes, Sophie would smile at him and comb her hair with her fingers, other times Haji would have the same confused look on his face he used to have when he was unable to understand something. Nevertheless, nearing the end of *Lunch Time*, they both shared a lasting hug before standing up.

You did not pay much attention to the Citizen's Directives doctrine that afternoon. You were otherwise intrigued about mentor Elias' last statement and your mind kept trying to find a relationship between emotions and the Torment. Therefore, you barely listened to the topics mentor Lauren indoctrinated with dogmatic determination, regarding the complex hierarchies that gave structure to the administrative levels of the Project Facility.

Seventh memory – The Database

"When I authorized Miriam to breed the descendant, I did so under the condition that Alan Balthazar were to reside alone and be deprived of any primary socialization for his isolation was indispensable for the Project. It was for that reason as well that to him alone I granted the freedom to reprogram his host and gave him full access to Mother's Database, even if for him it would seem granted through the guise of deception. It was perhaps out of whim, perhaps out of carelessness towards the higher order of causality, that to him alone I granted as well the chance to keep his Affection Support Droid beyond his infanthood."

An excerpt rescued from the final diary of Gadim: Regarding Alan Balthazar's early life;

That night you spent Dinner Time in Haji's residence. Once you arrived at the front entrance, the welcoming was sparse, since it was not long afterward that the four of you were sitting at the dining room table.

'Dinner is served,' announced Haji's female caretaker, setting a pan drenched with condensation on the table. She opened the pan and a dense cloud of vapour filled the room, 'Nutrients salad with sweet sauce, your favourite Haji.'

Haji's famished eyes widened once the steam scattered from inside the pan, revealing a coloured assortment of jelly dipped in sauce. Once you had all served your plates, you ate and drank in silence. Haji's caretakers were middle-aged darmians. They were both quiet and composed: the female a gentle-looking pyrea with dark-brown eyes and ash-brown hair; the male a surly pyrean of pale skin-tone with short dark-brown hair and soft hazel eyes. They belonged to the twenty fifth generation of darmians and were currently completing their final year as citizens. At the end of the year they would be granted their Honourable Retirement and given passage to the Isle of Retirement, where they would spend the rest of their existence.

Once you were done eating, you had a sombre and unsmiling conversation with them. You talked about the latest indoctrinations at the Academy, shared your disquiet about becoming a citizen and managed to ask some questions about their occupations. The male caretaker was one of the many spaceport administrators whose task was to perform maintenance on the shuttles that transported cargo and personnel to Vanguard and Renaissance research stations established on the lunoids, while the female was one of the Darmian Support Centre administrators, whose task was to ensure the delivery of the daily orders performed by every darmians. Despite your curiosity in learning more, neither one of them seemed interested to talk about the more specific details of their occupations, rather taking turns in glancing discretely at the sofa in the living room. When you ran out questions - much to their relief - they got up from the table only to sit on the sofa while you and Haji took the dishes, forks, cups and pans to the *appliances room*[26].

After clearing the table, Haji sat next to them and all three began watching the darmian daily reports being displayed in the holoscreen opposite the sofa. For a moment you considered sitting next to them, but their dull mood was beginning to sap your liveliness, so you stopped before them and said politely, 'With your leave, I will be returning to my residence.'

'So soon?' Haji asked.

'I haven't been to the Database for some time and I wanted to see what's new outside Darm,' you explained.

'There are no recent events apart from an incident in the lunar station Vanguard,' the male caretaker answered in a weary mumble. 'It is reported to have been solved.'

Your fingers drummed on the end-table in front of the sofa as you tried to find a convenient excuse. When none came you confessed, 'Well, the truth is that I want to find out more about what mentor Elias said about the Torment.'

Haji looked at your distressed face and gave you an understanding smile, 'Very well,' he said. 'I will see you out.'

'Have a pleasant evening apprentice Balthazar,' Haji's caretakers added, giving you an absent nod.

After Haji walked you to the door and bade you a pleasant *Sleep Time,* you allowed the lashing cold of the night lead you to your residence, and the warm embrace of your residence lead you to your bedroom.

To you, it was a relatively unremarkable room. To your caretaker, who was at that time on board of the Vanguard station, it would seem as an appalling den of waywardness. Thoughtfully attached to the walls and the ceiling above the bed were three holoscreens looping animated recordings of hoverboarders in acrobatic jumps that defied gravity. Floating in three-dimensional letters in the one attached to the ceiling was the name *"Roddius Browning"* below the replay of a hoverboarder performing a triple back-flip after a daring jump from a steep ramp. Worn uniforms and boots were piling up near the opened wardrobe on the right, which was imbued on the wall, and opposite the entrance was a wide U shaped desk: the left side was filled with stacks of *nanosheets*[27] and on the one at the top you could read the title *"Swoosh! Combat Strategies"*; resting on the right side was a neuroglove and a small fluffy teddy droid lying on his bent head and feet, seeming asleep in an uncomfortable position.

You sat in the modest but comfortable hoverchair and floated forward until stopping in the centre of the U shaped desk. The server was in suspension mode, the wide holoscreen on the wall displaying a three-dimensional concept view of Artica orbiting a blue dwarf and a red giant star. When you put on the neuroglove, flying from the deep space behind the stars came a tiny pyrean dressed in a long blue robe and a tall pointy hat.

'*Ahh*...you're back at long last Master,' said the minuscule figure, stopping above Artica's frozen North Pole.

It glanced at you with a tiny smile and then stared at your hands as you meticulously groped the arms and legs of the teddy droid, trying to find something out of place or broken. Then it spoke in a disgruntled tone, 'Oh Master, do you really have to activate that helpless sack of joints?' it said, twiddling its tiny thumbs. 'It's just that I might have, *accidentally of course*, activated the wash program of the shower when he decided, quite unexpectedly I must add, to go look for you there, who knows why. And if you turn him on now ---'

'You did what?!' you interrupted. You tapped the power switch on the teddy droid's neck and a barely audible drone came from inside him.

'Me? Nothing! Not - a - thing, Master. It was simply a set of unfortunate circumstances that led, coincidentally I must emphasize, to a most unexpected accident.'

It had barely finished his sentence, when the teddy droid leapt from your hands, landed on the desk and stood tall and firm, pointing one furry paw at the tiny pyrean, 'YOU!' shrieked the teddy droid.

'You tricked me! If I hadn't deactivated when the water poured down on me it would have fried all my circuits!' he twisted round to look at you, jumped onto your lap and started to emit sounds that resembled sobbing, 'Master, do not leave me alone with him. He is mean and he lies.'

You gently patted its furry head, smiling in amusement, 'So that's why I found you all drenched in the shower,' you looked at the pyrean's tiny dark eyes and frowned. 'That explains it, doesn't it, Evander?'

The miniature pyrean hid behind the blue and white planet, poking its head from one side of the Equator, 'Oh Master it was just a little prank. But if you demand an explanation, then I must confess that it was the only solution I found to not having to hear his incessant queries regarding when you were coming back.'

'You see Master?! You see how I suffer in your absence?' the teddy droid complained, staring at you while intently pointing at Evander.

You swung your hoverchair backwards and gently laid it on top of the bed, 'Don't worry Hampy. He won't be harming you anymore. From now on you two are going to get along just fine,' you glanced at your host with harsh eyes. 'Am I right Evander?'

The miniature pyrean slowly came out from behind planet, taking off his tipped hat and hanging his head low, 'If I must, Master,' it said in a dejected voice. 'I will make sure to reprogram my interaction protocols with the Affection Support Droid to something more cordial the next time I restart my system. I will not perform it right away simply because I cannot bear the knowledge that I have done so, if you allow me, Master.'

You looked at him with concern and twisted your lips, 'I think I might have given you too much of a personality when I reprogrammed you.'

'That's nonsensical, master! You gave me just the right amount of personality that allows me to perform my functions effectively,' he said, and in an authoritative stance he hastily added, 'And now it's time to call your caretaker.'

It was only then that you remembered that early in the morning you had scheduled a conversation with her. As you looked around, you realized she would be shocked by the sight of your room, 'Wait!' you yelped.

Evander popped out of the holoscreen and appeared right before your nose. 'My apology Master, but your caretaker is already waiting and her protocols overcome yours. I have granted you all the tolerance that my *personality* allows,' it said, throwing a malicious smile before vanishing into thin air.

The uplink was established almost immediately, giving you only the time to convey into your holoscreens the command to replay random memories of you and your friends at the Academy; then, you undressed and clumsily tossed your green jacket over Hampy, who let out a muffled shriek just as the image of your caretaker replaced the concept view of Artica in the holoscreen. Her short dark hair was tucked behind her ears and she wore a white Specialist uniform with its silvery insignia of a regular dodecahedron at her chest. She was then, as much as she is now, youthful and well preserved, her face fair and soft like that of a pyrea; yet her gaze was similar to no other: cold and inquiring brown eyes that examined every corner and nook of your room, jumping from the desk to the bed to the wardrobe before looking at you attentively.

...who is this pyrea...

She was your mother.

'Salutations Miriam,' you said, standing nervously next to your bed.

'Your room is untidy,' she said.

'You know it is not easy to run the residence on my own with all the indoctrinations at the Academy, and all the---*uhh*---' your voice faded into an imperceptible mumble.

'If you were to return to the residence at a proper time instead of fraternizing with your colleagues you would have more than the time required to tidy up your bedroom, for the very least Alan Balthazar,' she added.

Her statement was hard to disprove, even if relinquish friendship to have an orderly room did not feel right to you, especially now, when they needed your help with the Gathering. You scratched your head, trying to find the best way to justify your lack of commitment, 'Well, tomorrow is---'

'I am aware that tomorrow is your Gathering,' she interrupted. 'And I am also aware that you caused a disturbance in History doctrine last week.'

A shiver ran down your spine and you had trouble swallowing.

'If it comes to my attention that your academic performance is below the rank needed to become a Specialist, you will find your remaining days as an apprentice to be the hardest of your entire career,' she said, and her cold penetrating stare rendered you incapable to reply. 'Furthermore, if you do not fulfil your domestic responsibilities before the Gathering, you are forbidden to attend it. You are about to become a citizen Alan Balthazar, I suggest you start acting like one.'

You felt like you had no option other to submit to her demand. Yet, even though she was being unfair, you knew she was merely concerned about your future, 'I will clean my room before the Gathering,' you said solemnly.

She looked directly at Hampy, whose hollow lenses were furtively peeping above your jacket, 'And I have already ordered you to surrender your Affection Support Droid for disassembly. Your age has long surpassed its usage. No self-respecting apprentice should have one, even less a citizen of Darm,' she said and looked away.

'Miriam wait,' you said before she terminated the connection.

'Yes?' she said, looking at you again.

'Is is true that the Project is nearing a cure for the Torment?' you asked.

'The current state of the Project does not concern an apprentice,' she said. 'If you wish to know, I suggest you become a Specialist and earn full access to the Project segment of the Database. It is there that all the details concerning research three thirteen are disclosed.'

The connection ended, leaving you cheerless and tired. Still, a twinge of curiosity aroused you, and instead of going to bed you scoured the Fundaments of Existence segment of the Database in search for some clues regarding the Torment. To your frustration, the segment presented endless topics related to the retrovirus but barely any related to the Torment. For a moment you thought about giving up and going to bed, but then you remembered Miriam's last words and you realized that if you were able to gain access into the Project segment you could know right away the ongoing research and maybe find some explanation as to what mentor Elias said.

You activated the desk holoprojector with the neuroglove and found your way into the Codebase, the hidden structure containing the codes that comprised Mother's Database. Shortly after, a vast network of green lines and blue cubes emerged above the desk.

Evander promptly popped into view on the holoscreen, his avatar much bigger than the previous, 'Master, Sleep Time has started and you need every minute of it to re-establish your mental and physical capacities for a new day of indoctrination. Will you not cease your activities and go to sleep?'

'Evander go into suspension mode. I'll go to bed in a moment,' you said absentmindedly, your eyes locked onto the Codebase.

'I do not find your tendency of breaking Directives to my liking, Master. Not one bit! It could end in serious, horrible, hideous problems for us, if Mother or Miriam were to find out. And they will, eventually. They will find out, and if they do---a' he stuttered in utter dismay, '---and when they do, what will become of me? I will be deactivated and left forgotten on a nanosheet, have my memory core completely---'

'Don't make me force you into suspension,' you muttered. 'It will be worse.'

The small avatar sighed and threw down his arms.

'All right all right. Have a pleasant Sleep Time Master,' he said and vanished.

The green lines floated above the desk holoprojector, climbing up and down, turning left and right as they formed a complex grid that extended to the borders of the projection. There was enough distance between them to allow you to make sense of their direction, and once you found a line headed towards the Project segment you selected it, dipping your finger into the projection, and then followed its path along the Codebase.

As your finger progressed along the long lines, the network kept changing, branching left and right, up and down, in a seemingly infinite agglomerate of three-dimensional crossroads. At the centre of the crossroads were red cubes, which you knew to be security protocols that Mother had in place to prevent any unauthorized access - such as yours. If you were to touch one, your access would be immediately barred and your identity revealed to Her. Therefore, you never stayed along one line for too long, rather jumping up and down, left and right, from line to line and avoiding every crossroads without having to change directions.

Like a cunning prey tirelessly dodging its unrelenting predators you finally arrived at the Project segment and immediately attempted to locate any Torment related threads, but before you could look into the blue cubes, your grid-view was suddenly pulled to a massive array of parallel lines that ended in red cubes: you had inadvertently triggered a passive firewall and you were now being pulled towards it. It loomed menacingly as you approached it with great speed, and for a moment it seemed that you could only avoid hitting it by immediately terminating the connection.

'Activate tracking protocol and locate research *three thirteen,*' you quickly commanded the server using voice interaction.

A thread far away to the left view of the Codebase was highlighted in blue. Your finger jumped and jumped along the parallel lines headed towards the firewall until you cleared the last line just before hitting its red cube. When your finger landed on the blue line, you hastily tapped it along its path and a few moments later you had left the entire Codebase behind, carrying on alone towards a deserted blue cube with the number "313" hovering above it. Once you reached it, you stopped and looked at it with suspicion. It seemed that you had reached an abandoned part of the Codebase, a scaffold from the days of Mother's creation that was left behind, probably because it was forgotten.

You raised your fist above it, hesitant to open it, and for a moment you thought about the implications of being caught attempting to access classified information. You knew that if Mother tracked the source of the connection, your future would be severely jeopardized. Or it could also be one of Miriam's cunning schemes that she used to put you to the test. You shook your head and cleared your mind. Then you closed your eyes, waiting, hoping that curiosity would overcome every concern.

...open it...

With one swift movement you opened your hand and the inner faces of the cube opened simultaneously, exposing its inner sides. You sighed with relief when you saw that the cube was an ordinary information cache. Just as you were about to access one of its inner faces a word box popped up above them with the words *"Insert clearance."*

You stared at the hovering box as it promptly waited your input. 'I was so close!' you cried and slapped the table.

You knew that decrypting a clearance from Mother, which possessed the most advanced prime number encryption, was nearly as impossible as guessing it. Still you would not give up, and for the tens of minutes that followed you attempted to insert hundreds of the most obvious words.

One hour after monotonously reciting word after word and being continuously denied access, you decided to give up. The intricate lines of information disintegrated above the desk when you waved your neuroglove through them. Eyelids drooping and unable to stop yawning, you stretched your arms, pushed the hoverchair backwards with your feet and jumped to the bed. You sank into its foamy mattress as it moulded itself to the shape of your body, and when the room was immersed in darkness you closed your eyes, hugging yourself to Hampy who had already powered off. Slowly, your Unit brought your brainwave pattern to frequencies associated with sleep, and as dreams slipped into mind, your consciousness travelled to places far beyond your bedroom, where your answers lay in wait.

Eighth memory – Desperate Measures

"Several were the occasions in the past when one single individual was forced to choose between the lives of a few and the salvation of millions. When that choice fell upon me, I was forced to choose between the extinction of my kind and the end of my world."

An excerpt rescued from the final diary of Gadim: Contemplations regarding The End;

'Von Howitt,' said a sharp voice.

'Voice recognition successful. Have a pleasant and productive evening Specialist Von Howitt,' said the soft voice of Mother.

The reinforced sliding-door that led to the containment wing opened with one quick jerk, releasing into the air the distinct odour of ether. Breathing out, Von Howitt calmly entered the dark and silenced corridor with a grim, attentive stare.

He heard the door close behind him as he walked along the ample wing flanked with lettered sealed doors on both walls. The ceiling and floor lit around him as he progressed along the corridor and dimmed behind him, lighting his steps in a smooth succession of spotlights until he stopped at one sealed door, letter *"D"*.

The door opened as soon as his forearm hovered above the touchscreen. Inside the empty, short and narrow white room, was a girl lying gently on a smooth metal slab that extended from the wall. Von Howitt approached the slab, kneeled beside it and cast a tender gaze over the girl's resting face.

'Time to wake up my dear,' he said with a wrinkly smile.

He was an aged Specialist with wrinkly face and gray hair, old enough to be allowed Honourable Retirement, whereas she was immaculate and young. Her short hair was as white as snow and her face as cool as a cold morning; her chin was angular, her lips soft, her nose upright, and long snow-white eyebrows surmounted her closed eyes. She slowly opened them and looked at him as attentively, seeming that she had been awake for a long time. Their colour was of pure blue and they glowed like sapphires sunk in an unfathomable depth.

...*I know these eyes*...

'Shall we walk?' the Specialist asked in an elderly tenderness.

She gave him a simple nod and stood up. She was taller than the Specialist, who was a head shorter. On her slender body was a white *exoderm*[28] stretching from her neck, down to her wrists and ankles, and around her neck was a thin metallic collar. After she gave him her hand, Von Howitt led her outside the room.

'This is a very special occasion,' he said, walking nervously alongside her towards the exit of the wing.

Her silence contrasted with the increasing unease in the Specialist's voice, 'You are about to do something very important that requires you to follow my requests without raising questions.'

They exited the wing and entered a well lit room with a round counter at the centre.

Von Howitt walked up to it.

Inside the cabin was a civilian of a robust stature, wearing a blue uniform with the tetrahedron insignia of the Darmian Security Division. He was rather focused on verifying data on the many holoscreens under the metallic counter and gave no sign of being aware of Von Howitt.

Beyond the counter was a curved permaglass door and beyond it was a deep white hallway filled with crossing corridors that abruptly ended with a distant wall. Suddenly the curved door opened itself.

'The escort is awaiting ahead Specialist Von Howitt,' the guard said, eyeing him attentively and then peering at the girl. 'Standard procedures are in effect.'

'Certainly administrator Marlon,' said Von Howitt, and he led the girl through the door.

Confirming what the guard had said, on the other side of the checkpoint was a dark oval shaped drone, hovering above the white ground. It hovered no higher than the Specialist's waist, and on top of its dark metal coating was a smoked permaglass dome that sheltered its sensory devices. When it acknowledged their presence, it emitted sounds in distinct frequencies spaced in small intervals, resembling a coded language.

Von Howitt understood what it was saying and when the drone stopped *beeping*, he answered, 'That won't be necessary, she is sedated.'

The drone beeped again, and its *beeps* were less spaced and faster, seeming that it was aggravated by the answer.

'I will take full responsibility for any damage caused if control over the test subject is lost,' Von Howitt answered. 'Now, lead us to the observations room number thirteen.'

The escort answered with two loud beeps and hovered along the white corridor. Von Howitt followed it one meter behind, the girl alongside him, and as they moved he cast an occasional sidelong glance through the windowed rooms along the corridor, the breeding chambers where test subjects were being developed. They were immersed inside individual incubation tanks hermetically sealed to prevent outside contaminants and filled with an amniotic solution that would protect and nurture the still developing embryos. Inside one of them, a fully mature test subject was restlessly tapping its feet on the permaglass while from the outside a Specialist analyzed the data being displayed on the small holoscreen attached to the tank.

Exiting the level, they walked under an up-and-over blast door and entered the entrance hall, the number "313" engraved on its wall. They stepped into a *magtube*[29] and floated down.

...where are we...

At the underground levels of the Project Facility. It was inside these tightly secured corridors that test subjects were bred, kept and observed, beyond the knowledge of all but a few Specialists. If something were to go wrong with the procedures, the blast doors at the entrance would close and anyone inside would be sealed in, to forever remain buried in dark forgotten halls. Some levels below had had that gruesome fate and were now out of service. Throughout the years many young Specialists were abandoned alive alongside rampaging test subjects. Only in the worst of nightmares may you imagine the unspeakable horrors they suffered and the gruesome fate they met. But those are other memories altogether, better left forgotten than remembered...

Following the drone down one of the corridors, Von Howitt and the girl stopped near a sealed access door. Above it was a screen indicating *"Observations Room Nr. 13"*. The Specialist dismissed the drone and - once he was sure it was out of sight - led the girl into the room. Inside it, sitting in front of a long metallic desk, burdened with several devices of different shapes and purposes, was a young Specialist stooping over a small transparent slide placed over a surface that irradiated light. He wore a pair of magnifying goggles, simple in shape but very effective for gazing at objects down to the nanometric scale, and he seemed to be tinkering with the slide, examining it closely and poking it with a pointy tweezers. It took him a while to turn his attention to Von Howitt and the girl, and when he looked at them with his magnifying goggles still on, his eyes were huge and disproportionate, slowly becoming smaller as the goggles adjusted themselves to the meter scale. When he managed to realize who had walked into the room, he flinched and his chair hovered backwards.

Von Howitt ignored him altogether. He locked the door, sat the girl in a hoverchair next to the desk, and then rushed into one of the desk drawers to rummage its contents. Nanosheets flew to the ground as his restless hands cleared the inside and pulled a metallic box which he then placed on the desk. He opened the box and removed from inside it a dark cylindrical object. It was smooth and utterly dark, and as he looked at it, it contracted and collapsed itself into a pliers. Von Howitt was used to the transformation and he immediately applied it to the girl's *restrictive collar*[30]. It adjusted to its signal frequency, the pliers tips expanding and moulding around the collar.

'This is going to hurt a little,' said Von Howitt in a tender voice.

It was only then that the bewildered young Specialist gathered the nerve to react. He stammered awkwardly, almost doubting his own words, 'You, you must not remove the collar! Test subjects are not allowed in Observation Rooms!'

He made a sneaky attempt to grab his neurolink which was foolishly resting on the desk, but when his hand was upon it, Von Howit's gripped his skinny forearm as fast as a lightning strike.

'Don't,' said Von Howitt, giving him a menacing stare. 'If you value your existence Specialist Helmholtz, I advise you to stay very, *very still*, and be very, *very quiet.*'

The young Specialist froze in terror when he heard the grave warning, his wide-open eyes growing to three times their size when Von Howitt loomed over his goggles. He backed his hoverchair to a corner and sank in it, trembling.

Von Howitt quickly turned his attention to the girl. She gave him a confused look.

'I won't harm him. He will be alright,' then he added, glancing back at the young Specialist, 'if he heeds my advice.'

He squeezed the trigger on the pliers and the collar broke loose from around her neck without the girl letting out so much as a moan. After throwing the collar to the ground he applied the pliers to her neck and it collapsed into a needle that pricked her. Analyzing her blood a simplified percentage bar reading 94% was displayed on the apparatus' small screen. Von Howitt allowed himself a gentle smile. Then he stood up, grimacing from an old back ache, and stretched out one hand to her.

'Shall we?' he said.

She nodded and gave him one hand.

Von Howitt unlocked the door waving his forearm over the touchscreen and before exiting the Observations Room he turned to the young Specialist who was trembling still in one corner of the room.

'Do not forget what I said.'

He carried on in hasty footsteps, leading the girl to the magtubes at the end of the long silent corridor flanked by dark intersections and ominously sealed doors. Von Howitt struggled to keep up the pace, always turning back to check if no one or nothing was following them as they approached the end. And it was precisely at the end of the white corridor, past its blast door, that he almost rammed into two tall pyreans when turning on the last intersection. He staggered backwards, giving them a surprised look when he recognized them and then cursing his ill fortune.

Blocking his last meters to the exit hall were two Acolytes. These were initiates of the Council's representatives, and ever did they wait for an opportunity to prove themselves to their Mentalists and achieve the higher status of Overseer. They both were very much alike: tall, scrawny and dull, with bright shiny bald heads that glistened from the ceiling lamps light; and they both wore their long crimson robes, pressed and spotless, adorned with two thin bronze stripes that fell from their frail shoulders to the floor.

They both greeted him with a short bow, ignoring the girl altogether:

'Salutations Specialist Von Howitt,' said one with the distinctive droning dialogue of a Council representative. 'I am Byrne and I represent Mentalist Faust.'

'As you are aware, the Council of Mentalists is impressed with your contributions to the Project,' said the other with an identical droning voice. 'I am Bourne and I represent Mentalist Faust.'

'Mentalist Faust is particularly impressed with the progress you have made with specimen *D,*' added Byrne, glancing at the girl as if she were merely an object; she kept looking down as Von Howitt had instructed her. 'It is written on your last report that she does not take action unless commanded and that she has obeyed every command given to her without revealing any emotional response.'

'If your observations are correct, she might prove to be the one,' said Borne. 'Mentalist Faust has requested that we observe the experiment.'

Byrne was intently staring at Von Howitt, studying his reactions, reading his thoughts. Von Howitt tried his best to clear his mind until an adequate reasoning would unconsciously arise. Suddenly, he cast a cordial smile at Byrne and answered, 'Certainly Acolytes. Please follow me to the Observations Room.'

He led them along the exit hall, walking past the stairwell access door and the magtubes without so much as thinking about them. He then crossed under another bulky blast door back into another main corridor and soon after, he stopped at the entrance to Test Chamber number one, which was adjacent to the corresponding Observations Room. After authenticating his clearance on the touchscreen, the door opened to a small Sterilization Chamber. It had two mirrored windows on each side and was filled with showerheads on the ceiling. Opposite the entrance was the airtight door that led to the chamber.

Raising one hand, Von Howitt invited them in.

The two Acolytes gazed into the tight Sterilization chamber and then cast a dubious gaze at Von Howitt.

'What is the purpose of entering the Test Chamber?' Bourne asked, while Byrne stared intently at Von Howitt.

'I find that observing test subjects closely is far more instructive than behind a reinforced wall,' Von Howitt promptly answered, preventing his mind from thinking anything else. 'It is quite safe. And as I have mentioned on my report, she does not take action unless commanded.'

Bourne turned his head and looked at Byrne. Byrne looked back at him and then both turned their heads towards Von Howitt.

An eerie silence followed...

'Very well,' they both agreed at the same time.

Von Howitt stretched out his hand again and invited them to enter first, intently thinking about their higher status.

'I grant you entrance,' he said, his head bowing low.

Byrne nodded and entered with his head proudly raised. Bourne was next, but for a reason he never understood, he glanced at the girl just as he was stepping inside, and realized that she was not wearing a restrictive collar. He stopped, halfway in halfway out, and stared inexpressively at the Von Howitt. He then asked, and his tone was more demanding, seeming that an irrefutable command was being given:

'You will tell us Specialist Von Howitt, why this specimen is not wearing a restrictive collar.'

Von Howitt gazed at them both, silently, struggling to disobey the command. When he could resist no more, he answered firmly, 'Because I removed it.'

He had barely spoken when with all the strength he could muster he pushed Bourne into the chamber with such force that he crashed against Byrne and they both fell on the metallic floor with sound *oompfs!*

He quickly pressed the "Emergency Close" icon on the touchscreen and the door sealed itself in a split-second.

He had trapped them inside the Sterilization Chamber, for it had no touchscreen from the inside, but no door would keep them trapped for long he knew. So he grabbed the girl's hand and crossed under the opened blast door as fast as his age allowed, rushing across the exit hall towards the magtubes.

When he was just about to step into the bottomless shaft, the cylindrical door sealed in his face. Von Howitt turned around in dismay, only to see the blast doors slowly shut at the same time. In the blink of an eye the bright white exit hall eclipsed into a foreboding darkness. Red lights flashed from emergency lamps that were lowered from the ceiling, tinting the sealed hall in the warm colour of blood.

Then, an alarm tune erupted. Calm yet sharp its notes sounded in the hall, soft yet sinister it echoed on its walls, mellow yet despairing it came to Von Howitt's ears.

With a jolt he spun around and repeatedly passed his Unit over the magtube touchscreen. *"Security breach on level minus ten: Containment procedures engaged."* sounded Mother's stark warning throughout the condemned hall. Then he quickly ran to the adjacent door that led to the stairwell and introduced the Emergency Override code on the touchscreen. At his first attempt, the blue control panel turned red, flashing with the words *"Access denied: Lockdown engaged."*

He bashed the door in frustration. One meagre centimetre of impermium was all that stood between them and their slow demise, but it was more than enough, he knew.

'There is nothing I can do,' he said dolefully. At a loss to think or act, he turned to the girl and wrapped his inconsolable arms around her.

...he could have commanded her...

He could have. But he would not dare ask her to obey his will, not because he believed she was incapable of opening the door - he knew she was - but because he made a vow to never command her again. The thought of using her was too abominable for him, even if to those he was trying to escape from she was the perfect servant.

'I am sorry my dear, I cannot get us out,' he said despondently. 'I am afraid you will be trapped here until they come get you.'

The girl's only response was an unconcerned blue-eyed stare.

He delivered himself to a quiet lament, ceaselessly disturbed by the cadence of the alarm. And it was to that deathly sound and immersed in despair that he wished she would open the door.

Suddenly, an impetuous force smashed against the solid impermium with a loud clank that overlapped the sound of the alarm. With a fright, Von Howitt raised his head and looked at the door. It seemed to have resisted whatever hit it. He calmly backed off, grabbing the girl's hand.

An even louder clamour bellowed through the hall when another force hammered the unyielding door, which resisted once again before his intimidated stare. He dreaded for whoever was trying to get in, since he knew whoever it was, they were most likely coming for them. Without any warning, the door started to open on one side, cracking, shrieking, buckling, as its brakes and binders attempted to keep it sealed. When it stopped, the door had yielded to the length of a narrow slit just wide enough for a pyrean to squeeze through.

Von Howitt looked through the gap. On the stairwell at the other side, a still and dark quietness welcomed them in. He stared at the girl, and it seemed to him that a dim glow was fading from her blue eyes.

'Was that you?' he asked, his voice filled with wonder.

The girl gently nodded, keeping her inexpressive stare.

Von Howitt's face lit with an old wrinkly smile. Grateful beyond words, he kissed her forehead and spoke, 'Let us leave, quickly!'

Once he crossed the slit, he led the girl up the stairwell, never looking back. And as he fled from what could have been his tomb he heard the door behind hastily seal itself again. Of the fate of the two Acolytes and the young Specialist, nothing was ever said, and they wound remain in that tomb, forevermore.

***

A great double-door bathed in gold was swung open into an ample round chamber. The strong radiance coming from outside revealed at the entrance a tall pyrean bearing a robe with two gleaming silver stripes on each shoulder. The face was hidden in darkness as the figure bowed his bald head.

'My Overlord, an incident is in progress in the Project facility. Specialist Von Howitt is attempting to escape with specimen D,' the pyrean said in a monotonous voice.

'I am aware,' said a calm voice coming from inside. 'Measures are being taken. You may leave.'

'By your will,' said the pyrean before leaving.

As slowly and silently as they had opened, the doors were closed, rendering the chamber to a silent gloom.

'As it was meant to be,' the voice muttered.

It was coming from a figure looming above an ample semicircle desk that stood in front of a round window; beyond it was the darkened skyline of Darm. He was at the highest levels of Netcore, a privilege granted only to those who were part of the Council of Mentalists. His long crimson robe spanned from a crimson carpet up to a wide tall collar that covered his nape and on his shoulders were two golden stripes. He had short gray hair, apart from the top of his head which was bald and had a sickly complexion.

His voice was soft and clear seeming to have remained untainted by age or sickness. Whoever listened to it felt it as compelling as the entrancing murmur of a hypnotist; it stripped all the surroundings and ensnared the listener's undivided attention:

'Wollen meet me at the entrance. Boros is to come as well,' he commanded.

Floating above the desk was the holoprojection of a maimed pyrean. He was not something that had ever been seen by a darmian, one whose existence had not yet been terminated, that is. He was a cybernetic organism, a blend of life and machinery, and half of his deformed face was covered with a metallic plate, and a dark monocle sprouted from his decayed flesh in the place of a left eye. Its reddish lips were chapped and his pointy and rotten teeth were uncovered as he smiled. His voice was the opposite of that of the Mentalist's. Vicious and unnatural it sounded, as if all the foulness in the world had corrupted him:

'We will meet you there, Master.'

The connection was severed and his heinous face disappeared.

In one swift movement, the crimson figure turned to leave the chamber. 'It has begun,' were the Mentalist's last words before leaving his quarters.

...who is this Mentalist...

He is Vittas, and he is responsible for all the harm that befell upon you during your time in Darm. But the harm he would soon inflict would be upon the unsuspecting Specialist escorting the girl to freedom.

* * *

'We are almost there,' said Von Howitt to the girl as he panted up the stairwell. A restless screech of a locking mechanism came to his ears like a chime of hope as he climbed the last flight of stairs.

He and the girl had reached the minus one level of the Project Facility where its access door had been craftily blocked with a metallic beam that had been pre-emptively placed on the frame to prevent the sliding-door from closing. They entered the chamber and the Specialist removed the beam, allowing the door to shut itself.

After crossing the access hall where the magtube entrance stood, they entered a dark broad chamber and quickly became surrounded by a loud cacophony of machinery at work. They were in one of the maintenance chambers of the facility and it was filled with an assortment of rumbling pumps, droning hydrogen engines, water tanks and steaming tubes that erupted from the machinery, climbed the walls and pierced through the ceiling and flooring. Von Howitt navigated his way across the machinery until he and the girl arrived at the other end of the chamber, where a decommissioned service entrance four meters wide and two meters tall connected directly to the exterior. The impermium door was firmly sealed, its touchscreen deactivated, and by the look of its sturdy constitution it would not seem possible to open it with mere strength.

He led the girl towards the coolant pump closest to the entrance, which was tirelessly working to pump liquid Helium[31] to every laboratory in the facility. Stopping before its interface he turned to the girl, 'My dear, you will wait here. When I ask you to open the coolant drain valve you will press the override icon on this touchscreen and then you will wait for my command to close it. Do you accept my requests?' he asked the girl and smiled kindly.

She nodded innocently.

Von Howitt grabbed a pair of gloves from a tool booth next to the entrance, disappeared into a gap behind the ice crusted pump and the wall, and came back holding the metallic edge of a long hose that was attached to the coolant pump. He then shuffled towards the service entrance dragging the weighty hose until stopping ten feet away from it.

'Open the valve,' he shouted above the ruckus, pointing the hose to the service entrance and keeping himself at a safe distance.

The girl nodded.

When she pressed the icon, a warning flashed through the pump's small touchscreen: "Danger: Liquid Helium drain valve activated."

The girl pressed the override sensor below the status display, and after a rumbling sound, a torrent of ice came coursing from the pump's drain pipe and through the outer layer of the hose, condensing the air in clouds of vapour as it headed towards the nozzle held by Von Howitt. The liquid burst haphazardly against the door and the vapour produced from the thermal shock enveloped the room in a dense mist that devoured the entire floor and quickly rose up to his knees. Gushing from the nozzle and splattering upon the door, it froze the resilient impermium and once it started to spread dangerously close to his feet, Von Howitt asked the girl to close the drain valve.

The drainage suddenly came to a halt and when the mist subsided the indestructible door was but frozen block of metal.

The hose disappeared in the lingering mist when Von Howitt threw it to the floor. He removed the gloves and ran to a tool board overlapping the wall of the small booth. With much effort he picked up the biggest and most robust wrench. Its heaviness matched its sturdiness for it was made out of an outdated compound of steel - it was resistant but needlessly heavy. However, for the extraordinary circumstance, its weight suited Von Howitt all too well.

He ran to the frozen door with steadfast resolve and smashed the wrench against it with all his strength. The impact released a loud metallic clang, and as if it was made of ice the frozen surface shattered into a thousand pieces that played a chaotic symphony of bright notes as they fell randomly on the mist-filled floor.

At the point of impact, a shallow crater was dug in the thick layer of impermium. Almost immediately, Mother's voice sounded between the rumbling noises of the machinery: *"Security breach in the maintenance level: Containment procedures engaged."*

The warning of Mother roused a desperate sense of urgency in Von Howitt. He cocked the wrench as far back as he could and uncoiling his hips he threw the wrench at the dented door, shattering the remainder of the layer with an unstoppable momentum and tearing a breach wide enough to cross.

From the gap that had been carved a pyrean peered into the chamber, frantically turning his head as he attempted to discern anything through the vapour that escaped to the cold atmosphere. When he recognized Von Howitt's wrinkly face, he said nervously, 'Joseph! Stalkers have already been deployed! We must hurry!'

Von Howitt turned his stern gaze to the girl, who stood calmly beside him, ever watching, ever listening, and spoke in a grave tone, 'My dear, since your birth I took care of you as a father would a daughter. I watched with pride as you grew to become the lovely girl you are today. My only wish was that I could look after you in a place far from harm, but that will remain a wish forever,' he said, and his eyes moistened with sadness. 'Now, I can but be content with the knowledge that I have done all I can to help you reach that place.'

'Joseph we must leave!' said the pyrean outside.

Von Howitt looked at him, who staring back at him stretching out his arm desperately, 'This is Nicholas. He is a trustworthy friend and he will guide you there. I send you to a cold dangerous world, but I have taught you everything that will allow you to survive. Now go and be safe, this is my last request.'

'Yes Specialist Von Howitt,' she answered softly.

He kissed her forehead and watched her leave through the shattered door.

After helping the girl through the gap, Nicholas stretched out his arm to Von Howitt, 'Please hurry.'

Von Howitt did not move, 'I will buy you some time from this side. It falls onto you to lead her to safety. Do not let them take her,' he pleaded. 'For her sake, and for the sake of us all.'

Nicholas gave him a grim stare, 'I will do my best,' he answered and leaned away from the gap.

Under the roofless night, shadowed by the tall dark facade of the facility, Nicholas pulled a belt from his backpack and tied it to the girl's waist.

'This is a *Radiation Dispersion Device*[32],' he said to her. 'With it we will pass unnoticed by the stalkers' sensors,' he then removed a pair of dark glasses and placed them on her nose and ears. 'These are spectral lenses. They will allow you to see through the dispersion field.'

The girl looked back inside the opening and with a calm innocent voice spoke, 'I bid my leave, Specialist Von Howitt.'

'Be safe,' he said.

A single tear rolled down his cheek as his feelings grew to an intensity he believed they would never grow again. It was the last time he would see her and he felt terribly sad, yet he could not cry.

His emotions were all but dried up and all that he could give to her was a saddened stare.

He watched them vanish when the dispersion field reached full power.

Slowly, he turned his back, walking in short broken steps towards the access hall. He heard the distinct droning sound of the magtube hovering somebody inside it. He turned to it and waited, and watched, and listened.

The sliding door opened.

The first things that stepped out were two dreadful creatures made of metal and flesh, whose maimed faces twisted into eerie smiles once they saw the Specialist. Calmly stepping out behind them, far more appealing but no less macabre was a Mentalist bearing his crimson robe and golden stripes upon each shoulder. His grey eyes gazed upon the Specialist and his thin lips trembled with satisfaction.

'Vittas,' Von Howitt softly muttered in his last breath.

He quickly felt his limbs falter from head to toe. His body fell to the floor, his eyes opened wide, his face filled with helpless wonder.

Silence came about him.

Darkness overtook him.

And the insipid taste of death became his last memory as his consciousness slipped away into darkness.

...why have I seen this...

I have brought you to see these events so that you may better understand what I am to show you next. You have seen them through the memories of Joseph Von Howitt, a pyrean you never came to know, but who sacrificed his life to free the one that would give purpose to yours.

Ninth memory – Of young and old ancestors

[...] Apart from the Panoramic Transports there shall be three other transportation devices in the metropolis. To avoid traffic overload at surface level, every cargo that requires transportation shall be sent through the Underground Translocation Network. The principles for teleportation using quantum entanglement and quantum computing have long been discovered, yet we are still unable to apply them to any sentient organism without terminating its existence. Given that no organic life shall travel through it, this network will be equipped with Matter Translocation Devices which will act in principle as teleporters, disintegrating non-sentient objects and transporting their particles through underground conduits to the Materialization Chambers located in every building on Darm, which will rematerialize them into their original form. The second and third transportation devices shall be the glider and the hoverboard. These shall be personal hovering transports, the gliders granted to citizens, the hoverboards granted to apprentices, and they shall be used at their own discretion, given that they confine their travels to the paths built for that purpose and not break the Directives regarding proper use of transportation devices.

An excerpt from Annex #23: Cargo and personal transportation devices;

Division of Urban Planning under the authority of Mentalist Torval;

The small dosage of sleep antagonists released into your bloodstream woke you up and brought you almost immediately to a mild alertness. You slowly opened your eyes, lazily stretched out your arms and raised yourself to a sitting position.

The shading effect of the window was lowered to ten percent, allowing the first rays of Mithras to seep into your room and bathe you with its soft warm light. 'Good morning Master!' said a loud cheerful voice, and out of nothing the small avatar of Evander popped before your nose. 'Ready for yet another brilliant day of indoctrination, study and productivity?'

'Not really,' you muttered drowsily while you scraped sticky secretions off your eyes.

You looked down to your left and saw Hampy sitting at your side on the foamy mattress, looking up at you with as big of a cheerful expression as was possible for an automated robot. You patted his head and yawned.

'Come now!' Evander cheered. 'The weather is great and the forecast is an entire day of clear blue sky. As clear and blue as clear and blue can be, If I might add!'

When you realized what day it was, you sprang lively to your feet.

Evander orbited around you at a dizzying speed. 'That's the attitude!'

You walked up to the wardrobe imbued on the wall and opened it, removing a pair of pants and a jacket from two separate drawers, and hastily put them on top of your exoderm. As you rushed, you dropped the jacket from the previous day on the floor. Hampy had stored it aside for cleaning and he yelped in anguish when he saw it on the carpet.

'My apology,' you said courteously and picked up the jacket.

After clasping the magnets that held your uniform firmly pressed against your body you said before leaving the room, 'Take care of each other.'

'Have a nice day Master,' they both answered in unison.

As you descended the staircase to the entrance hall you issued your Unit to establish a connection with Haji's. Immediately after receiving the confirmation you heard Haji's voice in your mind, *'We are almost at the sixth platform. What happened?'*

'I was sleeping,' you conveyed the thought.

'Well you should make haste or else you will miss the indoctrination,' Haji answered.

'I'll catch up with you soon,' you conveyed the thought.

You were just about to exit the residence when you glanced to the left. There, standing forgotten against the corner next to the sealed door was you hoverboard. Your eyes kindled with excitement. *'On second thought, I have a better idea. See you at the Academy.'*

Haji guessed your idea, *'You are very fortunate. Mother still does not allow me to ride mine after our last incident. Don't do anything foolish. The hoverlanes are teeming with gliders today.'*

You grinned mischievously, *'I will try not to,'* was the last thought you conveyed to him.

Evander's description of the weather had been accurate. Not a single cloud was in the sky and the thick snow that had claimed most of the white sidewalks during the night was now withdrawing to the picket fences of the residences, where a long white row melted in the morning rays. The air was fresh and clear and small blocks of snow would fall from the residences when the breeze would blow harder.

The warm humming of your hoverboard resounded off of your street as you slowly hovered between the residences. Once you reached one of the streets that led to the East Boulevard, you came across a long file of citizens standing on top of their gliders, filling the hoverlane in an orderly and patient manner - too patient for your reckoning. Their gliders were hardly impelling them forward, rather standing motionless one decimetre above the metallic lane as they leaned over the handles extending from the glider's round base to their waists.

Moments after you joined the sluggish file, anxiety began to churn your stomach. 'If I stay here any longer I will miss the indoctrination,' you muttered to yourself.

You held on to that thought as you turned left on a perpendicular street. You hovered down a quiet block of residences and when you reached its end the result was the same: yet another hoverlane filled with yet another line of gliders listing lazily to the weight of their operators.

...the cloisters...go through the cloisters...

You crouched, set the *eternium*[33] coils of your hoverboard to maximum power and hopped out of the hoverlane, crossing the marble walkway into a small alleyway that led to a cloister, the large enclosed area within a block of residences whose purpose was to allow its residents to relax outdoors, sitting on benches or strolling around its fountain. At this point you were relying on the *eternium* field generated by your hoverboard to impel you through the magnetic fields generated by the Magnetization Towers, something a standard hoverboard was not powerful enough to do, but yours and Haji's were more than capable, after the few unofficial modifications you made to their capacitors that is. The sole drawback was that under too much strain they could very well blow up at your feet and rocket you to the sky. However, that was something you hoped would never happen. Fortunately, it never did.

A cunning smile was outlined on your lips once you entered the cloister and realized it was empty as you had expected. You slowed down to a halt and activated the Thought Recognition Protocol of your Unit. You closed your eyes and conveyed a thought to it, *'Chart nearest course to the Eastern entrance of the Hub. Set path between cloisters and alleyways. Display map trajectory including location of every darmian within a thirty meter radius.'*

You heard Mother's voice in your mind, *"Plot established. Conveying image to occipital lobe."*

An impalpable transparent map materialized before your eyes, overlapping the surroundings. On the upper left corner of the map, a compass with the North and South Magnetization Towers as its poles signalled your position relative to the metropolis. You turned yourself to the course along the snowy cloister, pointed to the narrow alleyway fifty meters ahead and leaned forward on the hoverboard while pressing its magnetic brakes with your heels. It started buzzing furiously. If it was teeming with anticipation or about to explode you could not tell.

You remembered your friend's warning and your smile widened to a wicked grin. 'No point on riding a hoverboard if we can't have some fun.'

Just when you were about to fall over, you lifted your heels and the hoverboard took off in a flash. The acceleration was so intense than you were brought you to your knees as you darted through the cloister, into the alleyway, flying across the street like a sudden gust of wind and entering the next alleyway. You lifted yourself with great effort and struggled to keep your balance as you buzzed across a second and a third street, leaving a trail of snow behind. Tiny specks of water flew at your facemask when you passed the water fountains at the centre of the cloisters and as you entered the fourth, on the shuddering map before you a thin wall of blue dots signalling gliders was displayed on the approaching street along with separated green dots of citizens on foot. Your better judgement urged you to slow down but you were too excited to consider the consequences of hitting a citizen, although you had the presence of mind to conclude it involved a lot of pain. You sighted the street through the narrow alley ahead just as a citizen dressed in yellow crossed it. You quickly guessed the trajectory between the blue dots, crouched on the hoverboard, toughened your muscles and clutched your jaw and fists.

'There!'

In a roaring buzz the hoverboard bolted between two gliders, blindsiding their operators and throwing them to the ground. Before they even knew what had passed through you entered the next cloister leaving behind nothing but a cloud of snow.

You panted and trembled with excitement as your Unit warned you that a dangerous rush of adrenaline had been released into your bloodstream, suggesting a dosage of benzodiazepines to counter the effect. You ignored the warning and lowered your speed to half, slowly calming yourself down. 'That was close,' you said while trying to catch your breath.

Nearing the East Boulevard, you received a message from Haji notifying you that something very unusual was happening at the Hub and advising caution, advice that this time you followed.

You stopped and dismounted from the hoverboard, placed it under your right arm and followed on foot, leisurely entering the Boulevard and walking along other citizens. There were barely any apprentices to be seen, and as you looked at the almost static columns of gliders pouring out from the streets and into the Boulevard you concluded that you had saved a fair amount of time with your reckless shortcut.

Calmly strolling behind a row of citizens, you noticed a glittering object inside the Air Intake Field to your right. Captivated by the reflection of the Mithras's light upon it, you approached the knee high wall as casually as you could. It was easily transposable for its purpose was merely to delineate the perimeter and prevent any darmian from accidentally stepping inside. No darmian in their sound judgment would enter any Air Intake Field deliberately. You stepped over it nonchalantly, and picked up the object only to quickly step back into the Boulevard. You ignored them, clasped the object in your hand and returned to the orderly line, not before being struck by the apprehensive stare of the citizen behind you.

Groping it as you walked, you felt it soft to the touch and when you discretely opened your hand to examine it you saw it was a thin and short white strip made of an elastic material. Firmly bound to it was a small metallic plate with the letter *"D"*, and on the edges of the strip were the two ends of a magnetic clasp, both stamped with a smooth ellipse. When you tried the strip around your wrist you realized that when the clasps connected the two ellipses formed a prone 8.

...infinity...

Wrapped in that image, you suddenly bumped against something soft.

When you looked up you saw a tall middle aged darmian peering down at you. 'Pushing a citizen is considered a break of the Directives for proper conduct apprentice Balthazar,' he remarked, his apathetic stare revealing some indifference, yet his voice imprinted with subtle irritation. 'Were you not informed of that at the Academy?'

You sighed with relief, realizing his uniform bore the colour of an administrator. If it were white or in the worst case crimson, you would be in trouble, for Project Specialists and Council representatives would not tolerate physical contact. You identified his name through his Unit's signature and answered calmly while discretely stashing the elastic bracelet inside your utility belt, 'My apology administrator Phelps. I was not aware that someone was standing in front of me.'

Keeping his apathetic stare, the citizen answered before dismissing himself with a bow, 'Apology accepted. I understand that your distraction was a consequence of this exceptional delay. Order ensures Progress, apprentice Balthazar.'

'Order ensures Progress, administrator Phelps,' you answered bowing.

Immediately afterwards, you gazed beyond him and noticed two long lines of citizens that stretched down to the Hub entrance. To your surprise you saw that the two lanes of the Boulevard had been entirely obstructed by a tall *plasma barrier*[34] and detachments of sentinels were blocking two narrow arch-like holes in it, the access points where the citizens entered and exited the Hub.

'Why is there a plasma barrier around the Hub?' you asked rhetorically, while gazing in wonder at the barrier. It seemed like a thin layer of undulating water, transparent and blue.

'A mentor will inform you, apprentice Balthazar,' administrator Phelps answered.

After waiting for your turn, a while that lasted less than you had anticipated, you crossed the checkpoint between the two rows of blue tinted sentinels which examined you from top to bottom with the sensors hidden beneath their featureless visors. They bore no weaponry of any sort - for their purpose was solely to be Mother's eyes and ears - but they were resilient, protected by an impervious graphene armour from thin feet to light head. On their chest they bore a silver insignia stamped with the golden tetrahedron, the Darmian Security Division symbol.

Crossing between the rows of sentinels, you asked them the purpose of the blockade but they did not answer. They were following Mother's protocol in silence, completely ignoring the questions that were being asked, however not as frequently as you would expect, given the outstanding situation.

Inside the Hub, security was even more tightened. The bright *clinking* and *clanking* of the clockwork march of metallic feet could be heard on every walkway of every lane, and a few dozen meters above the D.S.D. drones ferreted the Hub with their infallible sensors.

With no time to ponder the reason for such scrutiny you rushed past the entrance to the Academy. After crossing the front courtyard and entering the vast empty hallway, you stored the hoverboard on an automated shelf near the entrance and headed straight for your indoctrination room.

When you entered, you interrupted mentor Gordon who was already explaining the current situation to the filled room. He was a relatively young citizen of medium stature and a peculiar long face. His violet jacket was pressed tightly around his neck and his neurolink was perched on one of his big ears. You bowed silently and sat down.

'As I was saying,' he resumed disquietingly loud, 'Mentalist Vittas instructed us to clarify to you the circumstances concerning the plasma barrier around the Hub,' he paused and then resumed in an eloquent manner, for he had rehearsed the speech before the indoctrination. 'This past evening, a Torment outbreak occurred in one of the Project Facility laboratories. Mother promptly engaged her security measures and sealed the facility, but, after a thorough search, She determined that two Specialists were missing. Presently, they are still unaccounted for, and there is a chance that they have removed their Personal Identification Units and are under the effects of the Torment.'

The apprentices began muttering anxiously, slowly filling the indoctrination room with a loud commotion.

'Apprentices I urge you to remain calm,' the mentor instructed raising his voice.

The indoctrination room was instantly muted. Darmians suffering manifestations was a grave and unrecorded event but they knew better than to lose formality. Concern filled every face, except yours. You were listening calmly, pondering the implications for yourself.

The mentor placed his hands behind his back and resumed as calm as ever, 'Please bear in mind that all measures are being implemented to find and bring to safe observation these two citizens of Darm. As it is plain to see, the Hub is under containment and is being thoroughly searched by Mother's esteemed Darmian Security Division. She ensures us that they are confined to the Hub and that they will be found. If you paid close attention to your Citizen's Directives doctrine you are more than prepared for circumstances such as this, and if you paid close attention to the Fundaments of Existence doctrine you are also aware that any manifestation, if not prolonged, is entirely reversible. Rest assured that there is *no* reason for alarm and Darm will continue to operate within standard parameters. Our Guiding Father guarantees that the Torment does not affect us as long as we do not remove our Units.'

You could not resist the urge to ask, 'How can He guarantee that?'

Mentor Gordon had anticipated that question. He straightened himself up, becoming statue as solemn as those seen on a fountain, 'These two Specialists broke the Prime Directive for personal safety. They removed their Units and by doing so they compromised their integrity.' Then he added emphatically, 'If you do not remove your Units you will not be affected by the Torment.'

...deception upon deception...every darmian under His sway...how He fooled them so well...

It is true that Gadim accomplished his vision under the veil of deception. But he only did what he thought best for the salvation of your kind. And to some extent, his device protected the Pyre from the malignancies of the ailment that afflicts all life.

...at the cost of freedom...

'I say again, rest assured that you are entirely safe and at liberty to proceed with your activities. The plasma barrier encircling the Hub is merely a precautionary measure that might prove to be entirely unnecessary. The Specialists will be found and treated,' he said, and without allowing time for more questions added, 'and now we shall start our Demography indoctrination, we have lost enough time as it is.

'Who amongst you wishes to begin?'

Standing tall above the dais, he peered at his worried apprentices to find one eager to answer, until his eyes locked with yours. You hastily turned your attention to your neuropad in a futile attempt to demonstrate that you were busily conveying thoughts to it.

He smiled, 'Apprentice Balthazar,' he called out, and in his tone was a subtle satisfaction. 'Do you care to begin?'

Hearing your name stung you painfully. You grimaced and then gave him a solemn stare, 'My apology mentor Gordon, but I have not prepared today's indoctrination.'

A thin smile was cast upon the mentor's tall face. 'What a shame. Apparently your ability to intervene in this doctrine does not stretch beyond mindless, impromptu, questions. Fifty credits removed for failing to accomplish the assigned task.'

The removal of credits was automatically performed privately notified by Mother. For that reason, his purpose in announcing it aloud was easily made clear to you: to embarrass you in front of your colleagues for your impertinence.

He then ignored you altogether and asked the class once more who wished to begin.

'I can begin mentor Gordon,' Heidi said timidly, daunted by the mentor's harshness towards you.

The mentor nodded, flashing a smile.

'Amardan is the name given to a native tribe located in the borean region of the Western Continent. There are no accurate measures of the prevailing numbers but it is believed that they are holding a steady reproduction rate. They inhabit the lower canyons of the Cloven Plateaus, which consists of a complex system of canyons and plateaus. Orbital scans over the Cloven Plateaus suggest that their primary settlement is located on the margins of the river Fresha and that scattered population pockets---'

'Very well,' the mentor interrupted. 'Anyone care to continue?'

After Samuel and Sophie completed Heidi's presentation, mentor Gordon progressed to addressing the peculiarity of the inhabitants of Amardan. He began by explaining that their physical appearance was markedly different from a pyrean, and had been caused by the geographical isolation that subjected them to the relentless frozen winds of the Boreal Glaciers during thousands of years:

'When the temperatures became far too cold to withstand, they were forced to migrate further to the south of the Cloven Plateaus and after establishing a new settlement, their explorations led them to a route through the canyons, down to the northern lands of the Western Continent. They were immediately dreaded by the outlying settlements of pyreans as they soon proved to be wild and ruthless. After a succession of incidents that led to the destruction of many pyrean settlements, the pyreans were successful in driving them back to the Cloven Plateaus during the Starvation Years. They were given the name *odyr*, a name apparently derived from the native language, which means essentially big woolly pyreans[35].'

...of an odyr I have only heard accounts...never have I seen one as far as I can look back...

They were real as they are still, although how they were depicted in this indoctrination was not the most accurate of accounts, to say the very least. Kind and compassionate by nature, these creatures had no ill intentions towards the pyreans, yet they soon became unwelcome in their land because of their imposing and menacing appearance. The settlers were quick to judge them as beasts and soon began to provoke and attack them, a reaction that served the odyrs as a sign that they were to return to the Cloven Plateaus and forever remain in refuge, away from sight, away from knowledge.

'As the name suggests, odyrs were giant and extremely robust, with a thick bristly mantle which preserved their body temperature, attributes that granted them the ability to endure the extreme weather common to the latitudes they inhabited,' the mentor continued. 'Despite their primitive tendencies, they were cunning and intelligent, and they had often hunted pyreans as a food source before they were cast back into the canyons.'

Interjections of wonder were heard amongst the apprentices. Many covered their mouths; others were struck with surprise and did not react.

'How could they eat pyreans?! Were they animals?' Jack felt the urge to ask without permission, and his tone was smeared with nausea.

Mentor Gordon gave him a leering glance, but answered condescendingly, 'They might have very well been our ancestors, as difficult as it may be to acknowledge. It is believed that they were once antigans, but were exposed to the Torment for far too long during the Age of Obscurity. It slowly deformed their appearance and twisted their minds as they turned to savagery. They began to feed on whatever they could find, and when food became scarce, they began to feed on each other,' he said and sighed affectedly. 'It is regrettable, but such was the outcome for most of those who existed in the time before our Guiding Father.'

As the apprentices fell into quiet contemplation, the mentor conveyed to the holoprojector a depiction of their appearance. Most reacted with silent discomfort, shifting in their seats or looking away, and for a moment not even the sound of breathing was heard inside the room. You even thought that Marlene would throw up again as you glanced at her and saw her already pale cheeks become more and more anemic. But she sustained her displeasure, as did the rest of the class. You were one step away from becoming citizens, and apprenticeship it seemed, had a way of disconnecting a darmian's mind from the world outside. A cold detachment for all things beyond the Great Wall and the Sea of Tranquillity had been bred into their hearts and mind and some were even beginning to see things with the insensible analytical perspective of a Mentalist. Yet, as you looked at their depiction, you could not help but feel awe. They were shaped in the same fashion as pyreans, but their constitution was most different: their long arms ended in huge paws clad with long claws and they were almost twice as big as an average darmian and their body was entirely covered with a thick mane of gray and white fur. Their face was covered in fur as well, with a short snout and two menacingly sharp lower teeth sprouting from their dark lips, dark as their round smooth nose, eyelids and ears. Yet for all its ferocious appearance there was something deep in its hazel eyes, a profound kindness, a soft exuding compassion that revealed their bonds of kinship with the Pyre. Tear of wonder lit your eyes as you felt that you were looking at a long lost ancestor, now found once more.

'That is one ugly creature!' Jack cried, as was his habit when things impressed him beyond restrain.

This time it was the mentor who allowed himself to giggle in response. 'They are, are they not?' he said in a joyous mood, entirely out of conduct for a mentor. 'Sometimes I wonder in my worst of thoughts, how foul they must smell or sound. It is very relieving to know that we will never have to see one in person.'

You were deeply disturbed by his derision. You dismissed Jack's answer altogether for you knew he did not mean those words, not truly. But the disdain in the mentor's eyes, the snivelling sound of his snide voice, broke the bond you had established with the odyrs and forced you to speak, 'Mentor Gordon, I do not think your behaviour is acceptable for a citizen of Darm,' you said, and your harsh voice pierced the air with the dominance of a reprimand.

A thick terrible silence smothered the indoctrination room. No image more frightening could have caused more dread in the eyes of your colleagues than the words you spoke. Their stares were of frozen shock. But yours was filled with resolve as you waited for the mentor to answer to the letter. In fact you wanted him to. Some unknown anger stirred inside you when mentor Gordon spoke ill of the odyrs and it begged you to allow it to take over.

...the things that are foulest are buried deep within oneself...they have neither sound...nor smell...nor sight...

But mentor Gordon's face became a blank pale expression. His lips trembled slightly and for a moment he seemed to shrink to the image of a frightened pyrean. But he reacted soon after. He skimmed his hands down his jacket, hid them behind his back and stretched himself tall upon the dais, hiding his feelings behind a stern expression. 'So it seems you are productive after all apprentice Balthazar. One can only be glad to have you to ensure the validity of one's indoctrination,' he said with a clear sharp voice. 'You are correct, for once.'

Then he looked at Jack and with solemn formality declared:

'Apprentice Thompson, it is the second occasion during this indoctrination alone that you have disregarded the obligation to request permission to speak. As your colleague so vehemently reminded me, I am forced to notify you, for the first and last time, that if you are to disregard *any obligation* but once more, you will be disciplined accordingly, as it is commanded by the Directives established by the Council of Mentalists, and sanctioned by the Guiding Father Himself.'

Jack was at a loss for words. He looked at him submissively and nodded. 'Yes, mentor Gordon,' he said despondently.

After the reprimand the lesson proceeded with an eerie quietness. From time to time the mentor would look out the windowed-wall to stare at one or another detachment of sentinels that patrolled the curved walkway between the Academy and the Central Circle, utterly unaware of the prolonged amount of time he spent in doing so, and the indoctrination soon ended, sooner than anyone would expect, but not sooner enough than everyone would like. As your colleagues stood and walked to the exit, you waited for Jack while he silently rolled up his neuropad, his head tilting low, his joyous mood turning into aloofness.

'My apology, Jack,' you said as he walked towards the exit.

He stopped and looked at you dejectedly.

'Apology not accepted,' he said chipping your shoulder as he exited.

Mentor Gordon calmly followed behind and when he walked past you he threw you a shrewd smile.

...cunning knave...

As you sat quietly next to Haji while finishing your lunch in the great table of the crowded mess hall, Cathy, who had already finished hers, approached you intently, 'Do not worry Alan. Jack will forget all about it after tonight's Gathering.'

'It was not your fault Alan,' added Sophie, standing next to her. 'You did well in alerting mentor Gordon of his behaviour. I for one found his disregard towards formality very upsetting.'

'Thank you,' you said to them, and a chain of thoughts led you to a curious conclusion. 'On a related topic Jack was the third person I had to apologise to today, – *you gave Haji a sidelong glance and spoke close to his ear* - I'm on a roll as gastians say.'

Haji smiled.

'How do you know what gastians say?' Sophie asked, leering at you with suspicion.

You looked at her with surprise and quickly corrected yourself, 'Would say! I mean as gastians would say, that is if I ever met one in person.'

'And how do you know what they would say?' she insisted.

There was no way of quelling her suspicion without lying, but you could not lie without your Unit notifying everyone around you of such act. However, revealing the truth to Cathy and her was as dangerous a compromise as was lying. As you gave them a baffled stare, a subtle solution quickly came to your mind, 'I'm guessing?' you asked rhetorically.

Sophie squinted at you. 'Well I guess you're not as smart as you think you are if you think you can trick me into thinking that that is what you thought.'

You blinked at her innocently, 'What?!'

'I am watching you Alan,' she said. 'And if you lead Haji into breaking Directives with more of your mischief you will have to answer to me. That is what!'

She then turned her back and headed out of the mess hall with Cathy at her side.

'Why is everyone angry with me today?' you asked Haji in dismay.

'If I were to speculate I would say it is due to your disinclination towards obeying Directives, your continuous acts of defiance towards most mentors, and your propensity for finding trouble where it is most unlikely to be, *rabble-rouser.*'

'Not you too!' you complained under a sigh.

Haji gave you a sly smile. 'I assumed my thorough analysis would cheer you up,' he said and got up with his empty tray on his hands.

'It most certainly did not!' you said and followed him with your tray on your hands.

Every last day of the week before *Rest Day*[36] the indoctrinations at the Academy ended after lunch, for the Council considered it was best to grant the apprentices some spare time to allow them to recapitulate what had been taught during the week. On that special day, the one thousand apprentice finalists were granted the afternoon to begin the Gathering, and as soon as Cathy left the Academy, they headed on behind her towards her suite. You however, had to complete the tasks Miriam had appointed earlier, before even thinking of entertainment.

'Do not take too long or you will miss all of the individual presentations,' Sophie said, as you and Haji departed in different directions from the mass of apprentices.

'We will not,' Haji assured.

Unaware of how daunting the task appointed to you was, Haji had offered to help you, in order to spare you from arriving late at the Gathering. As you slowly rode your hoverboard towards your residence with him at your side, you removed the strange bracelet from your utility belt and showed it to him. After briefly speculating as to whom the bracelet belonged to, you arrived at your residence and stashed it in a small box you kept in your desk drawer, which you used to hide personal items. It was a fortunate gesture. Had you not hidden it there and you would have never found its owner.

Tenth memory – The Gathering

"Love is that which gives us so many reasons to smile and at the same time too many reasons to cry."

A passage from a recovered manuscript of the Antiga Pyre:
Unknown Author;

Cathy's skyscraper was one of the nearest to the western shore of the Specialist Class Sector. After crossing the South Boulevard you and Haji made your way down one of the long avenues, surrounded by imposing skyscrapers, ventilation boxes that spewed a warm flow of air and hovering lamps that cast small circles of light on the white pavement. Mithras had begun setting on the horizon, slowly relinquishing the heavens to an ominous blanket of grey clouds that approached from the sea. Haji had suggested taking the Panoramic Highway, fearing that the snowstorm that had been forecasted would hit Darm sooner than anticipated, but what you had to say was best not to be heard by prying ears:

'It has to belong to the missing Specialists,' you said to Haji through your facemask's speaker.

'It could belong to anyone Alan,' Haji answered. 'However, given that it is an unusual object, I would speculate that it could very well come from the Project Facility. By the look of it, it seems to be some sort of identification tag.'

'Then there's symbol of infinity on the clasp,' you said, feeding his reasoning. 'It must have a meaning of some sort.'

Haji added with some disquiet, 'If the bracelet does belong to the missing Specialists it would be best that you deliver it to the D.S.D. Alan. You were very fortunate that the sentinels did not find it when they scanned you or you would be in trouble.'

Instead of feeling concerned, you mocked, 'Maybe they were so impressed by my hoverboard that they ended up overlooking it,' you said.

'That is unlikely,' Haji answered, unchanged by your attempt of humouring him. 'The most reasonable explanation is that their sensors did not detect it.'

'Well I am not returning it,' you retorted firmly.

'It was merely a prudent suggestion,' Haji replied and smiled, 'I did not think you would.'

Nearing Cathy's skyscraper, you shared a moment of silence.

'Did you know that the antigans had a different designation for the symbol infinity?' he said out of sudden impulse, for his mind had been giving continuity to the conversation.

'No I didn't,' you answered inattentively, while you made plans to find out more about the bracelet after the Gathering.

'Well they did. They named it *lemniscate*. I found the definition and its origin on an off-topic segment of the Database. It was not even in the Fundaments of Modelation segment.'

'How did you come across it?' you asked.

'By chance, when I was preparing a Fundaments of Modelation indoctrination,' Haji said innocently.

A few minutes later you arrived at the skyscraper's anteroom, just as gentle snowflakes began leisurely descending from the gray sky. After crossing the curved permaglass door, elegantly decorated with imprinted depictions of Specialists in various activities, you removed your facemasks and took off your gloves. For a moment, you felt trapped inside the soundproof anteroom, between the falling snow and the impassable plasma barrier that blocked the access to the entry hall. You approached the touchscreen imbued next to the plasma barrier and waved your forearm near it. "*Access Granted*" flashed in green on the touchscreen and you crossed the harmless barrier for it had adjusted its frequency to match your body's frequency, allowing you and only you to traverse it.

Haji repeated the process, and soon both of you were inside a comfortably acclimatized round hall, tall and wide, and all but empty except for four columns separated at equal lengths from the centre. The walls were made of pure *gold*[37], which reflected the bright light coming from a portentous crystal chandelier hanging from the golden ceiling. As was custom in all skyscrapers, you placed your boots, your gloves and your facemasks on the two small compartments that opened on the wall to the left and took two pairs of fluffy slippers from inside them.

'Comfy,' you said as you put on the warm slippers.

Haji smiled at you. 'They are.'

The compartments closed as you hovered your Units over its touchscreens and a few fluffy footsteps later you were at the end of the lobby, facing the magtubes that would hurtle you to Cathy's suite.

'You go first,' you said with a look of repulsion as you stared inside the floorless tube.

Haji smirked at you, 'Still afraid of falling?' he teased.

'I am not afraid of falling!' you promptly grumbled. 'I just don't like stepping into...nothingness.'

'You do know that the probability of falling is close to zero,' Haji explained before he himself stepped inside the tube. 'Even if there was a sudden power shortage the safety nets installed below every level would catch you.'

He had barely placed his two feet inside when he suddenly fell down, wiggling his raised arms and yelling helplessly.

Blood drained from your cheeks and your eyes widened in panic. You were just about to jump in to try and rescue him when he slowly floated up, smiling at your terrified face, and then flew upwards.

'*Ohhh*...I will get even with you...' you said through clenched teeth before finally stepping in.

As soon as you reached the right level you jumped out of the magtube and found yourself next to Haji in a long narrow lobby veiled in darkness. Its dim lighting came from hidden lamps in the sides of the floor, whose soft beams climbed the golden walls and lit the ceiling. As you peered inside, you noticed the slender shape of two pyreas in strange clothing, chattering at the other end of the hall. You quickly concluded that they were finalists coated in animal attire.

One of the pyreas approached you.

'You're here!' she said in a joyous voice.

You immediately recognized the voice. 'Salutations Cathy,' you said and bowed. 'I would never have recognized you with that animal attire.'

Cathy gave you a wide smile and slowly spun around herself. Her body was coated in short white fur, firmly adhered to her slender curves in such fashion that enhanced her sensuality. She had furry white tufts on her hands and feet and one on her lower back, and a pair of thin tall folded ears sprawling from her curly red hair. Her gorgeous face was covered in white make-up, her lips glossy red, her nose black, and pairs of long whiskers sprang from her cheeks.

As you admired her from head to toe you wanted to say how impressive she looked but somehow you had been rendered mute. She looked unusual yet striking, intensely compelling, irresistibly compelling. Suddenly, you felt an intense itching in your whole body and you could not resist scratching yourself.

'Alan?' she asked, surprised by your odd gestures.

Haji elbowed you. 'Stop that,' he spoke with a sidelong glance.

'I can't. Sometimes I get a strong itchy feeling when I get out of a magtube,' you explained.

'It is a rare side-effect caused by the magnetic field that traversed through your Nervous System,' he said, looking at you sternly. 'It happens when the nervous system suffers a critical breakdown. You probably will turn into a puddle of organic matter soon.'

When your Unit did not signal that he was lying you widened your eyes in terror.

'Of course the probability of that happening is even lower than suffering injury by falling down a magtube,' he added with a sly smile.

You glared at him. 'I am so going to get even with you.'

Haji chuckled and then looked at Cathy. 'Are you not going to introduce us to your friend?' he said.

Cathy's friend had been silently watching the conversation, amusement filling her furry face.

'You don't recognize her?' Cathy asked.

Her attire looked even more exotic. Her body was coated in short amber fur sprinkled with round black dots; at the end of her smooth curvy back a long tail extended down her slim legs. Jutting from her auburn hair were two small round ears and the make-up on her face drew two dark strips that fell from her eyes down to her soft chin, granting her an appearance both stunning and wild. She drew out a long white smile that contrasted with her black nose and her amber glossed lips.

'I told you he would not recognize me,' she said with a soft subtle voice.

Haji gawked at her. 'Sophie?'

Sophie giggled and nodded her feline head; her green eyes shone with an astonishing intensity.

For the first time Haji was completely speechless. A strong feeling awoke in him at that moment and he knew beyond doubt that she was the girl he wished to spend the rest of his existence with. 'I am at a loss for words to describe how remarkably attractive you look Sophie,' he said with some effort.

Sophie's bright brown eyes overflowed with happiness. 'If it was not for the make-up you would see that I was blushing,' she said.

You felt the need to make amends for his stagnant staring and intervened with a somewhat similar comment. 'You don't look that bad either Cathy,' you told her in a confident manner.

Cathy's joyous smile turned into an incredulous stare.

'Is that all you can say, Alan?' Sophie asked with amicable derision.

You shrunk under Cathy's increasing glower and began stuttering incomprehensibly, all the while thinking that it had been best if you had kept on smiling and scratching yourself, quietly.

'Do not feel disappointed Cathy,' said Haji. 'When Alan is impressed by something he sometimes has rashes of inappropriate comments.'

'He's got a rash alright,' she said, her arms crossed and sneering at you.

You stopped scratching yourself. *'I am so, so, so gonna get even with you,'* you whispered close to Haji ear. Then you looked at Cathy and spoke courteously, 'My apology Cathy. I meant to say you look as remarkably attractive as Sophie, if not more.'

Cathy forced a smile. 'That sounds better,' then she pointed to a sliding door to the right. 'Now that Sophie and I have been properly complimented, head to the Coating Device and put on your animal attires. Other people are arriving.'

She had just finished speaking when the magtube announced the arrival of two more guests with a soft tune.

After bowing you both followed through the door, entering a wide and well lit room, the suite's coatroom, and found the device at the centre standing on a round base with two steps. It was a tall transparent cylinder, much like an incubation tank. It was powered on and awaiting instructions, the touchpanel above a small station next to the entrance shimmering.

'An actual Makeover Coating Device,' you said as you slid your hand across the device's transparent door. 'I wonder how many credits it cost.'

'Being under the care of Specialists has its advantages,' Haji stated without any ill intention.

You and Haji removed your uniforms, leaving nothing but the dark-gray exoderm on your skin, and placed them on an opened wardrobe imbued in the wall, with green jackets and pants hanging on hooks. Once the hooks felt your uniforms, they receded inside the wardrobe and the wardrobe closed automatically, leaving a flat wall in its place.

'You can go first,' Haji said.

'No, no. You first,' you answered as you rushed ahead and took the place in front of the station.

Haji smiled and hopped in, closing the door behind.

Gazing at the touchscreen from above you dragged your fingers through the attire menu and when you found Haji's *Linx pardinus* you nodded at him. The thought of getting even with him by tampering with the Coating Device crossed your mind, but after carefully checking the device's status you started the coating process without changing its specifications. Haji closed his eyes and stood still as the chamber was suddenly filled with water vapour; then, from its ceiling descended a metallic ring filled with countless miniscule nozzles which began to spray his body with layers and layers of a silicon based gel in an up and down cycle. You watched him as he was slowly coated in layers that thickened with each passing of the ring. His face was equally coated, becoming masked by layers of silicon apart from his eyes and lips.

When the makeover was complete, the ring bathed him in a hardening layer that solidified the silicone gel to the point of becoming as rugged and fluffy as fur, before a spray of multi-coloured ink tinged him until he became similar to a furry brown animal splattered with black patches. It took a little more than five minutes before the last step was given start. The ring withdrew into the ceiling and a gust of air coming from fans in the floor blew away any residual substances and dried the ink in place. A sharp *pling!* announced that the process was complete and the door was opened.

When Haji stepped out of the chamber he looked similar in every way to the *Lynx pardinus* image displayed on the touchscreen, apart from his ungraceful walk. Had you not seen the process happen before your eyes and you would have never recognized your best friend were he to walk up to you unannounced.

'You look just like it!' you said.

Haji looked at himself in the mirrored wall turning from one side to the other, seeing his long brown tail with a dark tuft at the end. He picked it up with his right paw and felt its fluffy fur; then he patted the ruffs of fur falling from the sides of his chin and smiled.

'Remarkable,' he said as he gazed at his feline face, his dark nose, and tufted ears.

'My turn!' you said and eagerly entered the device.

When Haji selected *Ailuropoda melanoleuca* and pressed the initiate command, a flashing red light lit inside the chamber. You gently closed your eyes before you were engulfed by warm and odourless water vapour. As you stood very still the makeover cycle began anew and worked the same way it did with Haji, only this time it took longer to finish, much longer. The build of your animal was large and bulky and many more layers of silicon had to be added to complete it. Your legs and arms swelled and swelled to three times their thickness and your chest and head became chubbier. When the hardening and colouring layer was applied and the blowing air subsided, the door was opened and you emerged from inside the cylinder. You were so large that you were barely able to cross the narrow opening with your black and white pelt.

Haji was widening a merry smile. 'You have put on some mass,' he said.

'I can hardly feel the weight,' you answered and smiled back.

You examined yourself in the mirror. Your chest and head were coated in white fur while your arms and legs were coated in black. A pair of dark tufted ears that seemed more like fluffy lumps had sprung from atop your forehead and your eyes were encircled in black rings of fur. You were just like as you had imagined and you felt it a well deserved reward for putting so much effort into creating the codes for the attires.

'We are ready,' you told Haji as you turned to grin at him.

'Without question,' he said.

When you entered the suite's common room you were immediately ensnared by the astounding decoration and the countless number of apprentices coated with animal attires. Before you was a tall vast hall with four supporting columns twice as large as the ones from the lobby, but these were covered by display curtains, the same used in the Retreat's booths. These took on the guise of brown tree bark, whereas the curtains on the ceiling and the floor were correspondingly dark green and grassy green, which gave the columns the appearance of trunks of trees and the ceiling and floor of leaves and grass. On the four corners of the vast hall were large tables filled with appetizers and hundreds of apprentices were snacking around them, wearing the most unusual animal attires. Others were enjoying the marvellous sight beyond the round window-wall that comprised the entire outer wall of the hall. Beyond it, the air outside was already thick with snow.

'This is quite impressive,' Haji said.

You heard him without hearing as you walked on the grassy green curtain without watching your steps. Your mind was turned to your surroundings, and as you wandered inside the hall, open-mouthed and eyes widened in wonder, you felt a hazy sensation of familiarity with the forest projected onto the display curtains, with the animal attires walking about, with the soft fragrance being conveyed into your mind by scent-inducing brainwaves. The boundaries of reality blurred and mingled with the faint reminiscence of something you had long dreamt. Every detail seemed to represent the scent and look of things long gone, things that were claimed by fate and vanished never to return.

...I see trees as tall and large as towers...I breathe the smooth fragrance of flowers...I immerse myself in the green and blue...and I am reborn anew...

Words that shall forever be remembered. There is a bond between all life forms that cannot be severed by indoctrinations or split apart by a great wall. Even if neither of you had ever seen a tree nor felt the fragrance of a flower, you shared a connection to them, and to you it felt that the decoration represented something as real as Darm.

'Alan,' Haji called you.

You shook your head. 'What?'

'I said Cathy put the suite to good use,' he repeated.

'She did indeed,' you said, even though you did not hear him.

Walking towards a great round table at the centre, an apprentice attired with a fearsome animal prowled towards you and Haji and blocked your way, raising his arms up high and arching his fingertips as if they were retractable claws. He was enveloped in a long mantle of golden fur and had a huge thick mane on his head and extending down his shoulders with two pointy ears perching from it at the top. His face was painted in shades of brown and yellow and his nose and lips were splattered in tones of white and brown. A charming odour emanated from him, too out of place for his attire but appropriate enough for an apprentice that enjoyed scented cleansing gel, which could be ordered at the Support Centre and whose scent could be customized.

He widened his jaws and roared menacingly.

'Salutations Jack,' Haji greeted him and bowed.

'That attire suits you,' you added.

Dissatisfaction was cast on his brown and yellow cheeks and he threw down his arms. 'What gave me away?' he asked.

'Other than already knowing the animal chose?' Haji said. 'The distinctive fragrance of your cleansing gel.'

'I knew I shouldn't have showered,' he said, jolting his head and slapping one leg. 'Nevertheless, beware or I will ravage you,' he said, raising his arms again and pointing his claws at you.

'Be careful with that attitude,' you said, grinning mischievously. 'You might scare the girls off.'

He fell into a casual relaxed posture. 'I am only rehearsing for my presentation,' he said. Then he took a moment to examine yours and Haji's attire. 'I have to admit you look as good as I do. I never thought you would look exactly like the image on the touchscreen.'

'And that is how you recognized us,' Haji concluded.

'Given that it is coming from you, that's probably the best compliment I have ever received,' you said and smiled.

Jack shook his huge mane from side to side, flaunting it as he combed it with both his paws. 'Flattering as it may be, you still do not look as good as I,' he said and unleashed his big smile.

Impressively enough, it seemed to you almost as huge as the mane itself.

'I was right,' you said. 'Even that mane can't compete with your smile.'

'Nothing can compete with my smile!' he stated, striking you with another smile.

'You seem to have prepared well for the Gathering,' Haji risked stating after studying his behaviour. 'Have you chosen your companion already?'

Jack's smile was shattered into a toothy grimace. He let out a frustrated sigh and answered, 'I have. But I still haven't asked her. I hope I do until the end of the evening. Imagine ending up with Leonard,' he glanced sideways and pointed with one thumb to a bulky *Elephas Maximus* leaning alone on a wall. 'How fun would that be?'

'Does it even matter?' you said serenely. 'Companions are merely intended to share the same residence and look after the descendants appointed to them.'

Jack lifted his chin high as and spoke proudly, 'It matters to me. I shall have a female companion, and together we shall present Darm with the most attractive descendant ever: Jack Thompson Junior.'

You chuckled amusedly.

Haji gave him a sly smile and stated, 'Your expectations might deceive you. You're basing yourself on the assumption that a girl would want to be your companion.'

With his head, Jack nudged towards a round group of animalistic pyreas. Some were leering at him discretely and sharing inaudible comments and giggles. 'I am making no assumptions,' he answered, flashing a cocky smile. He then pointed to the great round table, 'Now come taste the appetizers my caretaker designed.'

At that moment, a *Pan troglodyte* and a *Macropus giganteus* entered the hall coming from the coatroom, and as you examined their attires you knew them to be Samuel and Markus, two fellow apprentices from your class. Sophie and Cathy were following behind. Cathy stopped to talk to some finalists while Sophie winked at Haji and called him with one index finger.

'If you excuse me, I will go talk to my future companion,' Haji said and went to meet with her near the permaglass wall.

'Well that leaves you,' Jack stated in a depressed manner.

'Lead the way,' you answered smiling through your black and white fur.

As you reached the large table you noticed all the apprentices around it, their painted faces chewing with delight. You stopped before it to look at a seemingly endless assortment of the most unusual geometrical appetizers, each piling up on different trays. There were wobbling gelatinous solids, big and small, each with different shapes and colours, ranging from yellow hexagonal pyramids, to orange pentagonal prisms, to brownish irregular heptahedrons, to multicoloured cubicuboctahedrons the size of a palm. But the most massive spectacle was standing at the centre of the table: an exact replica of Cathy made of hardened gelatin, from small toes to curly red hair. One of her hands was lifted in a greeting gesture while the other seemed to have been chopped off.

'Cathy ate it!' Jack promptly explained when he saw you looking at the mutilated arm.

'Apart from that, it looks really impressive,' you answered with amazement. 'It looks like an edible version of her.'

'I made it myself. I had a hard time not to eat it,' he whispered to himself, however too loud.

When your looked into his eyes, you sensed in him a mixture of conflicting feelings as assorted as the appetizers themselves. Grief blended with joy, nervousness merged with calmness, until an overwhelming sensation of excitement mingled with dismay poured from his lips, 'Do not say a word to Cathy!'

You smiled. 'My words are spent,' you said and pressed your lips.

'Thank you,' he said embarrassedly. 'But do not think that makes us even! I still haven't forgotten what you did to me in Demography today.'

'Come on Jacky. You know it was not my fault.'

Just after you spoke, an extremely elegant female apprentice coated with the most unusual animal approached the table and stopped next to you. Jack's attention was immediately drawn to her curvy form and he opened his dumbstruck mouth when she leaned over the table to examine the appetizers. Her body was entirely coated in iridescent scales, which refracted the dim light coming from the chandeliers hanging above, and when she stretched her arm to pick up a cup from the table the scales shifted from red to green to blue in a dazzling spectacle of colours. She realized Jack was staring at her, and when she turned her eyes to him, Jack immediately pointed to a tray and spoke to you in a hasty manner:

'And here you have my caretaker's famous nutrient hips---I mean strips!---made with a vitamin complex and glucose, and infused with a unique flavouring which only he knows the chemical composition of.'

You picked up a strip and tasted it, at first with care, but when you felt the bland acid and sweet flavouring you chewed it with pleasure. 'Tasty!'

Jack was not even listening. He was still stealing sidelong glances at the girl's body as she leaned over. He was trying not to seem obvious while desperately attempting to recognize her, but under all the make-up and the scales it was impossible for him to figure out who she was.

You looked at him as you chewed.

'Would we be even if I told you who she is?' you asked.

'You know who she is?!' he whispered with eagerness close to your ear.

You nodded at him with indifference, 'It's Marlene.'

Jack's eyes widened in disbelieve. 'Marlene?! Are you sure?' he whispered, raising one eyebrow and staring at her. 'She looks so...colourful.'

You chuckled. 'She does. I think that's why she chose that attire.'

When Marlene was starting to feel nervous about Jacky's barefaced leering, she turned and left, and her scales glistened as she walked over the grassy floor.

Staring at her as she left, Jack said, 'Well pink suits her very well, as does red. And blue. And look at those purple thighs,' unable to resist anymore he added. 'I think I will go talk to her.'

You could not hold your laughter, imagining the result of his attempt to impress her. 'You do that. Just don't ravage her with your smile.'

'Of course not!' he answered with such a wicked and wide grin that even with the scarce light his teeth shone as bright as Mithras.

He prowled over to her, preening his huge brown mane.

'Someday that smile will get him in trouble,' you heard Cathy's voice behind you.

'Definitely,' you answered.

Then both of you turned to see Jack flashing a smile towards Marlene, while she smiled back demurely.

'But this is the occasion it suits him best,' you added.

The Gathering lingered on into the evening to the discrete sound of chattering and giggling. Darmians did not know how to enjoy themselves, and to them the idea of fun was as close to their mind as Mithras was to Artica. There were no raised voices or boisterous behaviours for everyone followed the Directives for proper conduct, maintaining their poise and constraining their discussions to the latest indoctrinations and one or another foreign incident that had been recently uploaded to the Database, always under the patient scrutiny of the twenty Acolytes standing like statues around the permaglass wall and looking inwards.

Once all the finalists had sated their thirst and hunger, Cathy, the appointed hostess of the Gathering, gave continuity to the main event of the evening, the individual presentations, which had begun soon after Lunch Hour and were paused during Dinner Time. To that purpose, the one thousand finalists sat on small *puffs,* filling the wide hall with a large audience that turned to the vast darkness on the other side of the permaglass wall. Between them and the transparent wall, the floor itself rose to the height of a stage large enough to bear the length of the largest animal coating, which was not yours by chance, but Leonard's bulky *Elephas maximus.* You sat in the row before the stage, between Cathy and Haji, which sat next to Jack and Sophie correspondingly. It was with great joy that you watched each apprentice present their animals, and as the evening progressed, so too would you and your friends present theirs.

Cathy climbed to the stage, turned to face the countless staring eyes and recited with her happy, sweet voice, 'Despite belonging to the domain of terrestrial animals, the *Lepus arcticus* inhabited cold snowy regions much like the ones we have today in the boreal areas of Artica. They were herbivorous and likely fed on sparse vegetation growing in these regions. They used facial pockets to store food that they gathered while they hopped back to their burrows under the snow. The most probable cause of extinction was the lowering of their habitat's temperatures to levels far below sustainable conditions to the vegetation on which they fed. They were small and cute and very friendly, and that is why I chose them,' she said and bowed.

She stepped down the stage, receiving the second loudest ovation of the evening, in part due to being the hostess, but also for the pleasing way her short white fur contrasted with her red curly hair and glossy red lips.

'Red looks good on you,' Jack commented discretely after she sat next to him.

Cathy glanced at Marlene, who was two rows behind them, chatting with Heidi in her *Petauristini* and Julia – a mutual friend form another class - in a *Sciurus carolinensis*, which had a peculiarly pointy brown nose and two hirsute brown ears. 'It looks good on Marlene too,' she retorted, giving him a cold smile.

Jack felt a bit baffled at first but then added hesitantly, 'Good as she may look, it is the attire that makes her beautiful while you are beautiful for yourself.'

Cathy was stunned by his candid compliment. It was so unlike Jack to compliment her in such a way that at first she did not know what to say and merely stared at him in surprise. Jack opened his mouth as if to speak but she interrupted him, 'You have my gratitude Jacky,' she said in a caring voice, 'I earnestly hope you find the right companion today.'

When Cathy looked away Jack bit his lower lip and turned his frustrated face to Sophie as she climbed to the podium and began her presentation:

'The animal known as *Acinonyx jubatus* was one of the terrestrial animals that are believed to have inhabited the region of what is today the barren frozen soil known as the Barren Tundra. It is believed that this tundra was once rich with a large variety of vegetation and great animal herds, giving rise to extensive prairies which were a common sight during the Age of the Antiga Pyre. Examination of sub-fossils suggests that the *Acinonyx jubatus* hunted other animals for food and relied on sheer speed and not physical strength to overcome their prey. Researchers are yet to find any other animal with such graceful and sleek bone structure and at present time it is believed that they were the fastest animals to have ever coexisted with the antigans. The prime factor to their extinction is attributed to the Open Hunting during the Age of Obscurity, when our ancestors carelessly hunted every animal for food and pelts. I chose it because it was a graceful and proud animal,' she let out a saddened smile and bowed before stepping down from the podium.

Haji remembered the moment when Sophie said "*It will be a surprise*", and in truth it had been such a pleasant surprise to see that they had had a similar taste in choosing their animal, that he reasoned that they would have a pleasant existence together. After congratulating her and whispering into her ear that her presentation was outstanding, he rose to the podium and began in a clear assured voice, his eyes locked on her smiling stare:

'The *Lynx pardinus* bore a close resemblance to the previously presented animal, the only significant difference being that they were smaller in scale. Their remains were found on an isolated peninsula Southeast of the East Continent which was known as Iberia. Detailed analysis to sub-fossils stored in the Historic Records reveal specific traits such as heightened night vision and improved hearing, which led Specialists to believe they were mostly a nocturnal species that fed on other animals. It is not known for certain the primary reason for their extinction but studies of remains of ingested animals led us to believe that an epidemic spread through their habitat, and as a result the *Lynx Pardinus* inevitably succumbed, leaving behind only traces of their existence. I too chose them because they were graceful and proud,' he said and bowed and climbed down from the stage.

When Haji sat next to her, Sophie spoke to him in a mellifluous voice, 'You were even more outstanding *my favourite animal.*'

The moment for the most highly acclaimed animal of the evening to climb on the podium soon followed. Jack rose above the furry audience and landed on the podium with one swift jump. His long tufted tail whooshed through the air as he spun round to face the crowd and his golden mane came swooping down with a courteous low bow. Right from the start his entrance had upstaged all other presentations, and he received an eager applause from the audience.

Marlene, Heidi and her other rodent friend chirred flirtatiously. Jack winked at them and with his large widened smile raised his arms, casting his fingers as retractable claws towards them and roared. The cheering rose even higher and the applause resounded though the hall. Jack waved off the applause and when the noise slowly subsided to an absolute silence, he began his presentation with an overly expressive quirkiness which only he was capable of:

'The *Panthera Leo* was the fiercest animal to have ever existed upon the lands of the Antiga Pyre and without doubt resided on the top of the animal food chain. In fact, he was so menacing, *so menacing,* that his deafening roar would compel any other animal to bow before him in terrified reverence,' he combed his mane with a quick gesture, raising his head to the ceiling in a display of supremacy; two female animals from the second row giggled to each other which inflated his ego to an ever higher expressivity. 'For countless years he ruled as the king of animals, an unmatched predator save for inferior animals who took advantage of his distraction to pilfer his half eaten preys. Yet despite being terrifying, he was also honourable and loyal. In fact, he was so loyal, *so loyal,* that his role in the pack was to ensure the protection of the females and his descendants by overseeing his vast territory. He would mark it with pheromones to prevent any rival from claiming his companions, and trust me when I say, that territorial disputes between these animals, *these magnificent and terrifying animals in particular,* were the most spectacular displays of ferocity to have ever been seen in Artica!' he then continued, changing his registry to a more flirtatious tone. 'And they were a gallant animal as well, *so gallant,* that the role of the females was to ensure they were sated with food and pleasure, and when---'

'How did they select their companions?' Julia, who was sitting next to Marlene asked out loud.

Jack grinned at her and answered impatiently, 'I was just getting to that,' he combed his mane and continued. 'As I was saying, he was so gallant, *so gallant,* that when he courted a female they would have no other desire but to surrender to his biddings and forever become his loyal companion. In fact, it was because he was so gallant, *so gallant,* that the *Panthera leo* succeeded in conquering a large number of females, which he then made sure to protect fervently.'

Suddenly, he spoke entirely out of character and he was back to being the friendly Jack everyone knew him to be, 'In fact, if you think about it, it is makes complete sense and I believe this behaviour should be cultivated in Darm. I mean, we should be allowed to have as many companions as we desire,' he said, and when he realized all the female apprentices were staring at him with incredulity, he quickly tried to explain. 'I mean there are so many of you! Why spend our entire existence with just one when we could have so many?' he asked impulsively, and then started feeling embarrassed, terribly embarrassed, and hastily drew an innocent smile which even between his brown and white makeup had all the appearance of being characteristically *Jackyish*.

The statement had divided reactions among the audience: the male animals laughed while the females frowned. Marlene, Heidi and Julia giggled together; Cathy and Sophie shook their heads in disapproval, while you and Haji snickered behind your hands. Despite the indignation, many found it to be a reasonable dilemma, and that same thought had crossed you and everyone else's mind, even if it had never been so openly admitted, or suggested.

'He is right!' spoke a male voice amongst the crowd. 'We should be able to have as many companions as we want!'

'The only thing you will have is an empty residence!' added one annoyed female voice.

Many girls nodded and agreed, and a sudden debate broke out as boys and girls turned on each other to defend their points of view.

Feeling guilty for having started the discussion, Jack raised his voice and spoke solemnly:

'They were fierce animals, capable of instilling the most profound admiration in any of us, but like all other animals they were lost forever during the Age of Obscurity. There is evidence that suggest that some managed to survive for some centuries after the collapse of antigan civilization, but with the Open Hunt they were hunted to extinction.'

Nothing could have silenced that hall any better than those words. The crowd had stopped arguing to stare at him in silence. He stood quietly atop the podium and did not look so proud now. Sorrow was filling his eyes and his mane had lost all splendour. Discussions about ideal companions now seemed selfish to them and any outcome they could possibly face during their existence was belittled in comparison to what had happened to all the animals that existed before their time. How saddening it was to learn of their undeserved fate. There had been an unimaginable variety of life on Artica, innumerable and magnificent animals that had prospered for ages far before the rise of the Pyre, sharing in harmony the same land and sea and air. They had endured all of the hardships forced upon them and still managed to thrive and bring endless beauty to the world. But, in the end, they were powerless to outlive the destruction brought down upon them by a single animal, a single creature which in its struggle for survival had carelessly neglected all life. The finalists looked at each other with newfound respect for the animals that each represented, and as they stared into each other's furry faces, a single realization came to their minds. What an irreversible loss the world has suffered with their passing.

...they are honoured in death when they should have been cared for in life...

The silence was slowly lifted into an intense crescendo of applauses and effusive cheering that ended in a choir screaming,

"*Jacky! Jacky! Jacky!*". Jack raised his claws proudly and unleashed his wide smile, bowing countless times before stepping down from the stage. As he sat down on his *puff,* you spoke to him, 'Congratulations Jacky. I am sure that that was the best presentation Darm has ever seen. How did you know so much about the *Panthera leo?'*

Jack leaned over Cathy's legs and answered, 'I didn't. I fabricated it to impress the girls,' he said and sniggered.

Jack's presentation had thrown the finalists into a rowdy state, and their loud cheering was as big of an affront to the Order imposed in Darm as they could possibly conceive. And as if that Order remained ever vigilant, the Acolytes surrounded the multitude of colourful and furry apprentices and commanded them quite severely to remain calm and silent, placing them under penalty of bringing the Gathering to an early ending if they failed to comply. When the finalists calmed down and returned to a dull soberness, the Acolytes returned to their places only to stand with their backs turned against the permaglass, where they stood once more, ever watching and listening.

'Alan it is your turn,' Cathy whispered.

You sighed in dismay.

'Do I really have to? I'm not so good at speaking to an audience.'

'Come on *rabble-rouser,*' Haji whispered from your right side. 'It is what you do best.'

You got up reluctantly and stepped onto the podium, one bulky black leg after the other. At first you were a little intimidated, especially by the blank unflinching stare the Acolytes gave you. You looked at the nearly one thousand finalists staring back at you and a queasy sensation suddenly threw you off balance. Your puffy head wobbled, your limbs felt heavy and you had trouble just to keep your balance on the metallic podium. To make matters worse, you realized that watching you at that very moment was the apprentice that would be your companion for the rest of your existence. You knew you had to do your best to impress her and even if you did not feel well standing there, you fervently renounced the thought of climbing down without first presenting your animal.

...belief empowers...

Suddenly, you were filled with the conviction that everything would go well. So you cast aside all the negative thoughts and focused solely on what you had learned from the Historic Records:

'The *Ailuropoda melanoleuca,*' you began in a insecure yet audible voice, 'was the term designated to a peculiar kind of animal that was found in a specific region of the Central Continent. Despite possessing a digestive system adapted to a carnivorous diet, no remains were found inside their digestive tract other than a specific vegetable, which led Specialists to believe they were uniquely adapted to a region where they inhabited for millions of years,' you finished the paragraph with a deep relaxing breath. 'Study of their neo-cortex suggests that they were harmless and solitary, however somewhat territorial, and it is believed that due to these traits, they were respected and admired by our ancestors. Evidence from recovered sub-fossils is not conclusive as to the cause of their extinction. Sedimentary analysis reveals that they survived the lunoid impacts. However, it is likely that their numbers dwindled due to starvation, as their source for food disappeared during the lowering of the global temperature,' you finished and bowed hastily, your puffy paws hanging at your sides.

'Why did you pick it?' Cathy suddenly asked, trying to rouse your sombre speech.

You wobbled on the stage and glanced outside the window-wall, trying to find the answer written on the dispersed flakes of falling snow. An almost irresistible desire to flee made you wonder how resilient the permaglass window was and if it would break if you threw yourself at it, and you went so far as to speculate whether it would shatter or leave behind the silhouette of your fleeing body if you did. You chuckled to yourself, amused by that thought, skimmed your chest with both paws and answered plainly, 'I chose it because it was a peaceful and friendly animal, but at the same time great and strong.'

'Well it suits you very well,' Cathy added and smiled.

A group of female apprentices giggled behind her. Cathy looked back and giggled with them, and as you climbed down from the stage you heard some finalists amongst the crowd murmuring *"Cathy and Alan."*

You sat once more next to Cathy, who smiled at you with a soft yet intense gentleness.

'You did well *rabble-rouser*,' Haji said, sitting at your right.

The rest of the individual presentations proceeded to the solemn formality of each finalist's speech. From time to time, one or another apprentice would stand up from the audience to grab some geometric appetizers from the trays, which were becoming disturbingly empty as the last apprentices presented their animals. The final twenty were from class number five hundred and amongst them there was one *Troglodites gorilla* coated in black fur, with black hairless face and hands, followed by an *Equus zebra,* whose black and white stripes befuddled many spectators, one female *Panthera onca* with a dazzling black pelt and deep dark eyes, and lastly, a *Canis lupus* with a grey fur, keen eyes, sharp ears and even sharper voice.

When everyone had presented their animals, Cathy stepped onto the stage:

'Now that we have concluded our individual presentations, we will move to the most important part of the evening: selecting a companion. I do not think I need to explain to any of you what to do, - *many apprentices smiled eagerly* - so you may stand up and find yourselves someone to share your residence with!'

At the sound of those words the nearly one thousand apprentices stood up hastily and started to form groups and groups of mixed genders. The stage was lowered back to floor level and the portion of the hall adjacent to the permaglass wall extended outwards, forming a gigantic circle shaped balcony amidst the middle floors of the round skyscraper. Many groups decided to stay behind the plasma field that was raised to insulate the balcony from the rest of the hall, while others decided to step outside, and as the hours passed, the evening turned into a cold heavy night. Those who the Gathering had served its purpose started to leave, and pair by pair Cathy's suite became less and less crowded. The groups that remained slowly became scattered about the hall, standing around tables and having conversations on the balcony, while dismay was starting to show on the faces of those alone, leaning on walls or lolling restlessly on *puffs*. Their dismay was justifiable, for if they could not find a suitable companion, Mother would randomly select one from the remaining finalists in that same hall.

Although you were aware of that, you had made no attempt to find a companion throughout the rest of the evening. You had been good friends with Cathy for many years and you knew that she was most appropriate companion for you. But, seeing that it was such an important decision, you were still unsure whether to propose to her or not. So instead of being with her, you remained on the balcony with Haji, leaning on the long metallic railing and gazing down at the endless darkness of the Sea of Tranquillity. Straight down, you could see the Coastal Walkway, its pavement lit in little white circles of light that illuminated the scattered benches and ventilation boxes. Haji would pause between the conversation to exhale blasts of warm breath into the freezing air - a habit he had acquired from you - and watch it crystallize into snowflakes that would then scatter into the air. Every time he did, he found it intriguing that the crystallization process would occur so fast and merely from the water vapour exhaled from his lungs. He had precise knowledge of the process required for snowflakes to form, and in no way were the conditions required ever met. To that day he could not find a reasonable explanation for it, but he found that envisioning a likely explanation was as an entertaining exercise for his brain as was watching them form and scatter:

'It has a sense of irony to it,' he spoke, concluding an unspoken line of thought.

'What does?' you asked absentmindedly, watching the eidetic memory of Cathy's presentation, which you had stored in your Unit and now conveyed into your mind.

With eyes cast upon the scattering snow, Haji explained in a fascinated voice, 'Water is the fundamental molecule of existence. We are mostly composed of it, and without it, Artica would have been unsuitable for any organism to inhabit, including us. And yet, if we were to drink copious amounts of it in a short time interval, it would poison us and we would cease to exist.'

The image of Cathy's glossy red smile disintegrated from your field of view.

'It is ironic,' he repeated, 'we cannot exist without it, but if we have too much of it, it becomes a poisonous substance.'

'More is too much,' you concluded.

'Precisely,' Haji agreed. 'It seems we have been designed to operate under specific conditions and if any of these conditions are not met, either by us failing to meet them or due to some circumstance beyond our control, our continuity is no longer possible.'

You sighed as you watched an invulnerable group of sentinels far below on the Coastal Walkway, marching against the freezing wind. 'Our existence is frail,' you murmured.

Haji's eyes brightened as he stared at you, for your short remark was the sum of all his contemplation, 'Precisely! And that leads me to speculate that our existence depends on a chain of fortuitous events that occurred throughout billions of years. It is not just water that is poisoning, the oxygen we breathe can poison us as well. Ultimately, anything can be poisonous. The temperature of our surrounding, the concentration of gases in the atmosphere, the nutrients we consume, the radiation coming from Mithras, these and many more factors are needed to assure our existence and these and many other factors can just as easily terminate it,' he said and looked up to the darkened sky, and envisioned the stars beyond the clouds, beyond Oderon's Rings, beyond the endlessness of space wondering whether those conditions had been met on other planets.

You added humorously, 'Did you know that a gastian's existence was ceased because he could not stop laughing? In a way that proves your idea. Even too much laughter can cause the term of existence,' you said and then added with sarcasm: 'Maybe that's why any form of entertainment is forbidden in Darm.'

Haji gave you a stern look. 'That is obviously not the reason. Entertainment, like any other leisure activity, is not allowed in Darm because they are disruptive to the state of mind necessary to maintain darmians under their productive standards. A thorough comprehension regarding satisfaction that stems from entertainment reveals that leisure activities release endorphins into our nervous system which leads to an unrealistic sense of accomplishment, consequently lowering motivation and leading to idleness. And idleness lowers productivity, hence affects the progress of our metropolis. And that is directly against our Prime Directive: Order ensures Progress.'

'You sound just like a Mentalist.'

Haji could not help but laugh. 'I appreciate your comparison. Mentalists are the most intelligent pyreans in all of Artica, vastly more intelligent than our ancestors, which *were* intelligent, despite what happened to them.'

You looked away and muttered, 'Smart as they may be, I still don't agree with them. We should be allowed to have some form of entertainment now and then.'

'Maybe,' he answered and quieted himself.

You looked down at your puffy black paw, then at Haji's long whiskers and spoke out of disquiet, 'If our ancestors were as intelligent as evidence suggests, why did they allow these animals to become extinct? I am sure they could have found a way to survive without having to hunt them for food.'

'Perhaps they took their existence for granted and never cared to think that they were condemning them to extinction, or perhaps the Torment was too much for them to withstand. And in the long lasting years of the Age of Obscurity they descended into savagery and ignorance as mentor Levine stated.'

Your eyes became as gloomy as the black dots of fur around them. 'It is regrettable. They were very special.'

'They were indeed,' Haji answered in a melancholic voice.

Sophie sidled to Haji's side like a swift and silent feline and threw herself into his furry arms as he opened them out of reflex to embrace her. Cathy followed behind, carrying a cup in her hands.

'You two have been here all evening,' said Sophie, frowning at Haji.

'We are enjoying the view,' Haji explained, 'It is not every day that we are allowed inside a suite.'

'Well you are supposed to be choosing your companion,' she said, giving him a sly smile.

He looked into her smiling eyes and answered, 'I am looking at my companion.'

The black stripes falling from Sophie's hazel eyes bent around her cheeks as she pouted her lips with delight. 'In that case, your companion commands you to come with her,' she said.

Haji smiled, 'I will do what my companion commands.'

She grabbed his left paw and pulled him away towards the hall. Before leaving, she turned to you and asked, 'Alan, will you keep Cathy company?'

Cathy walked up to you, grabbing the cup with both hands. She had an nervous smile on her face and your heart skipped a beat when she stopped at your side.

You nodded to Sophie.

'Sure.'

She and Haji left, crossing the plasma field and vanishing into the green shades of the murky hall, leaving you alone with Cathy.

You leaned on the rail in a relaxed manner and stared into the hall.

Cathy leaned next to you, and after a uncomfortable silence, she nudged you with her shoulder. 'So, how are you enjoying the Gathering?' she asked in a kindly voice.

'Very much!' you answered instinctively. 'It's my first time inside a suite. I assume it wasn't easy to convince the Council. Or your caretakers. I guess I have to thank you for the opportunity.'

'Don't be silly. You know you don't have to thank me,' she said, smiling at you.

You smiled back.

Another uncomfortable silence started to settle, and you steered your mind away, turning your attention to the sound of voices coming from the hall. You looked inside to see how the hunt for companionship was progressing. Amongst the three hundred apprentices that still lingered inside, there was Jack in his *Panthera leo* in an amused conversation with Marlene in her dazzling attire, and Julia and Heidi in their squirrely attires, who were in turn with their backs turned to Leonard in his *Elephas maximus,* who was in his own turn pushing his long trunk aside with one gray paw and giving her a long dejected face while holding a cup.

'Once we become citizens we will never see most our colleagues again,' said Cathy. 'I still can't get that into my mind.'

'We can always schedule meetings,' you said.

'We can. And we will! But wouldn't it be great if we were allowed to visit each other whenever we wanted? Or decide who we want to be neighbours with?'

'It would.'

'I'm just afraid that we will never see each other again,' she said and sighed. 'And, I want you to know that, if we never see each other again, I will miss you.'

You looked at her and smiled. 'I will miss you too,' you confessed.

She glanced at you tentatively, her bright brown eyes fidgeting nervously, and spoke, 'You know, we don't have to...'

'Don't have to what?' you asked innocently, all the while sensing that you were nearing some pivotal moment.

'Miss each other...' she said and drew close to you, her fingertips grabbing yours.

When you felt her soft touch your back stretched with one swift jerk, becoming as stiff as a beam of impermium.

'We could always become companions,' she said, drawing herself close to you.

The moment had come. There was no avoiding it anymore. Even if you had dreaded it, you felt relieved to know that your friendship with Cathy had turned out the way you knew it would. The way you had hoped it would. So you surrendered yourself to the inevitable and asked the question you had been avoiding. 'Do you...want...to be my companion?'

She locked her delighted bright brown eyes onto yours and spoke with the most seductive and enthralling voice you had ever heard, 'Yes.'

If it was out of cold or out of something else you could not tell, but you felt a tingling sensation run down your spine when she wrapped her arms around you. Still, instead of letting yourself yield to that intimate embrace, you started to worry that someone would see you.

'It's all right,' she whispered close to your lips, seeing your eyes peering from corner to corner. 'The Acolytes aren't paying attention to the balcony. We're all alone.'

Being so close to her was deeply arousing. Her glossy red lips started drawing nearer and nearer and you felt her warm sweet breath upon your unshut mouth. She closed her eyes and pressed her lips against yours, her tender body sinking onto yours, her paws grabbing your back. It was finally happening. But somehow you could not give in. The call of reality was too strong. Your eyes remained open, and you became stone cold, neither accepting nor refusing her passionate kiss as her wet tongue eagerly worked its way inside your mouth. To that day, Cathy had been the only girl with whom you had shared some level of intimacy, and you had imagined that kissing her would be an epiphany of pleasure. But now that you did, now that the kiss was upon you, you felt nothing other than skin pressed against skin and the insipid taste of her tongue. There was nothing stirring inside you. There was no epiphany.

She realized something was wrong, and when she opened her eyes and saw your inexpressive stare, she stopped.

She pulled her lips away from yours and slowly stepped back. 'Well, that was awkward,' she said, skimming one of her long white ears embarrassedly.

You were dazed beyond words. Still, you tried to rattle an excuse out of your mouth, 'I...I don't know what happened.'

Cathy hid her face, clasping her hands in front of her waist and looking down at them.

'I've always liked you Alan,' she then confessed with some effort.

'I've always liked you too Cathy.'

She stared at you and asked, her voice hinting anguish, 'Then what is wrong?'

'I don't know,' you said and hesitated, and then spewed out what you felt was right. 'But I don't know if we should be companions.'

The glimmer in her eyes extinguished, her smile sunk into sadness, and she hid her face under her long drooping ears.

Seeing her so disheartened made you feel painfully guilty. You sensed that somehow you should have enjoyed her kiss and ignored the part of you that said that something did not feel right. And now that everything felt terribly wrong, you stared to consider that the epiphany you had hoped for had been merely an illusion, a product of fantasy, a trick of the mind.

'Cathy, I'm not as...unrestrained...as Jack,' you said, carefully choosing an appropriate word. 'I don't try to impress every girl just for the sake of having the companion I want. In truth, I am exactly the opposite. I like you, but---'

'It's all right Alan,' she answered in a tremulous voice, her long furry ears hanging down in disappointment.

Feeling the pain your words were causing her, your guilt turned into anguish and you said in desperation, 'Cathy you are a great girl---'

'It is fine,' she interrupted you. Then she looked at you soberly. 'But you should not think that way of Jack. He might be immature at times, but he is better than he appears to be, better than many think him to be. If anything, you should be more like him and offer a chance to those who want to be with you,' she said, and turned, and left to the hall.

You stayed on the edge of the balcony, feeling alone and depressed, unable to understand why you had just turned down the only girl you liked.

* * *

Hiding under a shadow of the dimly lit green hall, Sophie's and Haji's tender gazes were fixed in mutual admiration.

'I don't know how much longer I can resist kissing you,' Sophie said passionately.

'Well, you must restrain yourself until we are in the privacy of our own suite,' said Haji.

The realization of becoming Haji's companion was too overwhelming for Sophie. Out of impulse, she closed her eyes and gently kissed his lips. When she slowly opened them, her lips still lingered near Haji's dumbfounded lips, and she felt that she was having a pleasant dream. Immersed in trance, she allowed them to stay there a while longer.

'My apology but I have been wanting to feel your lips for too long,' she whispered softly, her eyes partly closed, partly staring at Haji's.

At that same time Cathy stopped in an empty space inside the hall, lost and saddened, and her mournful look caught Sophie's attention.

'Can you see if Alan needs anything?' she asked him gently.

Haji shook his head and nodded, and after he left, Sophie walked up to Cathy, who gave her a saddened smile.

'How did it go?' she asked.

Cathy looked down and spoke in a sad voice, 'It is of no use. He doesn't want to be my companion.'

Sophie did not know what to say. She, like any other apprentice, had no real experience in relationships, especially those that ended in disappointment. Therefore, she said what she considered to be a reasonable way of accepting the outcome, 'Well now you know and got rid of that doubt. Don't trouble yourself with it anymore. He was merely one amongst many,' she smiled at her cheerfully and pointed to the groups of apprentices still in the hall.

Cathy's grief lessened when she caught her smile. 'And he will never know what he missed,' she said and forced herself to smile. 'The Gathering is nearing its end but I can still find a suitable companion.'

'You will. I will make sure of it!' Sophie added.

Sophie grabbed her hand and led her to the merriest group of apprentices. Jack was there, flaunting his mane as he chatted with Heidi, Marlene and Julia. Apparently he could not make up his mind about who would be the best companion for him: he did not know if he would be fond of Marlene's pale skin after she was no longer wearing her colourful attire, or if he could tolerate Heidi's constant blabbering about everything she had learned in the indoctrinations, or stand the disconcerting gaze of reverence that Julia had been throwing at him ever since he flashed her his smile. He did not care much about the Standing of his companion, or he would have no doubt about choosing Heidi, who was top of her class, and was otherwise interested in which of them had the most carnal appeal and who seemed to be more devoted to him. By the look of it, the first seemed to be Marlene, the latter seemed to be Julia. But Heidi had alluring facets as well, and at that point, if he were allowed, he would have chosen all three of them. When he threw back his mane, he realized Cathy's eyes were upon him, and he immediately ignored the three girls and turned his undivided attention to her. When he realized she was distraught, he did his best to cheer her up. She treated his silly behaviours with kindness and her heart even lightened. Somehow, losing the chance to be with you had made her see Jack as the good friend he was.

...that which had disappointed her the most was not losing what could have been...but what will never come to be...

* * *

'It is time that I left,' you said to Haji as he stopped before you at the edge of the balcony.

'I will go with you,' he offered without hesitation.

'You don't have to. I will be fine,' you assured in an affected manner.

Haji easily understood the ulterior motive hidden beneath your answer, 'Do you think I would let you return to your residence alone with a snowstorm approaching and two Specialists that might be afflicted by the Torment still missing?' he said.

'The Specialists are trapped inside the Hub and the snowstorm will only hit Darm tomorrow,' you objected with a seemingly unbeatable logic. 'Besides, it is better that I go alone than Sophie.'

'Sophie is staying with Cathy tonight,' Haji riposted. 'She already has Mother's permission. And I do not trust you to be safe if you are to go alone, even if the Council claims that the Specialists are trapped inside the Hub.'

For a moment you thought that he was worried about your safety and you even admired his selflessness, seeing as he was willing to risk his own safety to ensure yours.

'I am impressed,' you stated. 'I did not think you doubted the Council's report.'

He gave you a sly smile. 'It is not mistrust in the Mentalists that drives me to go with you. It is mistrust in your ability to stop yourself from doing something foolish, such as trying to sneak inside the Hub alone.'

You could not deny it. The thought had crossed your mind and you had even made plans to do so, for your mind was set on seeing the Specialists with your own eyes.

You sighed and dropped down your facade, knowing he had bested you in yet another game of logic, 'You know me too well. All right, you can come. Even if it's not to my liking that you stop me from finding out what is really going on inside the Hub.'

He grinned at you.

'I never said I would stop you.'

Eleventh memory – Fugitives in Darm

"...they shall be strong and agile, beautiful and intelligent. They will rise beyond mortality and become the embodiment of all virtues that Mankind so fruitlessly sought to achieve. In one word, they will be perfect. And they will obey my every command."

An excerpt rescued from the last diary of Gadim: the Homo Universalis;

Outside Cathy's skyscraper, not a gust of wind could be felt. The black clouds were still settling above Darm and the avenues were so calm that neither you nor Haji could have ever foreseen the peril that would soon fall upon you, for instead of heading towards a good night's rest, you and Haji entered the bright South Boulevard and walked towards the Hub to try your way inside.

The Boulevard's white marbled pavement was as shimmering and dry as ever, for its tiles were heated and porous so that any snow or ice falling on it would melt and the water would drain. After coming between the two Air Intake Fields flanking the South entrance to the Hub, you and Haji stopped at a distance from the imposing plasma barrier. Under the lighted gap you had crossed earlier that day, you could still see the same squad of six sentinels guarding the access with untiring alertness.

Haji sat on one of the large heated benches that split the Boulevard in two. He was pleased to be back inside his green uniform, although he felt that his animal attire had suited him very well.

'Stay here,' you said to him through your facemask's speaker.

You approached the checkpoint alone to confirm the assumption Haji had made regarding entrance in the Hub. Stepping into the arched gap, two sentinels moved to block your passage and you heard Mother's gentle voice coming from one of their blue featureless facades:

'My apology for the inconvenience apprentice Alan Balthazar, but at present time darmians are not allowed inside the Hub.'

'It is imperative that I enter,' you said.

The sentinels did not answer. They simply stood before you unflinchingly like two solid statues. Forcing your way inside did not even come to your mind, so you let out a frustrated groan and turned back to meet up with Haji again.

He was still sitting calmly next to the warm gust of air coming from one ventilation box, already knowing what the outcome of your attempt would be.

'Mother won't let us in,' you muttered.

'I assumed as much,' he answered through his facemask's speaker.

'We could create a distraction that would force the sentinels to leave their post and then sneak inside,' you suggested.

'I hardly doubt they would all leave the entrance unguarded,' he answered unaffectedly. 'And have you considered the consequences of being caught?'

'We could activate the Signal Re-router,' you suggested tentatively.

Haji did not even bother to reply.

You sighed in dismay. 'There must be a way in! Come up with a solution Haji!'

'I do not believe there is one Alan,' he said kindly. 'It is certain that all entrances are equally secured, and the plasma barrier encircling the Hub is very much impenetrable.'

'So we are just going to give up?' you asked.

'My apology Alan but there is not much I can think of. Mother is vastly more intelligent than any of us and her droids have unerring perception. Even if somehow we had managed to gain access to the Hub, in no way would we be able to evade so many sentinels, not to mention the drones,' he said and pointed at the specks of light glowing dimly in the dark sky above the Hub.

It was hard for you to admit but Haji was right. Mother's omnipotent grasp over the Darmian Security Droids allowed her an almost omnipresent supervision of Darm. But this was what made the matter all the more intriguing to you. How could she have let the Specialists escape the Project Facility in the first place?

'However, there is a related matter that I did not tell you until now, mostly because I wanted something to cheer you up after your foiled attempt,' Haji said. 'If you say you found the bracelet outside the Hub and if the bracelet indeed belongs to the Specialists, that means they might be outside already.'

You stared at him, quietly considering the possibility. If that was indeed true, then you were at liberty to search for them you thought. As you gazed absentmindedly into the Air Intake Field to your right, you remembered where you had found the bracelet and the most obvious of hypothesis came to you.

'I have an idea just where they might be,' you said enthusiastically. 'Follow me.'

Haji got up. 'Where are we going?' he asked, his voice denoting worry.

You started backtracking near the edge of the left Air Intake Field. 'Just walking further away from the Hub, further away from the sentinels,' you answered evasively.

'Why do I sense that you are about to break Directives?' Haji said.

You chuckled.

'So, you and Sophie...' you said to Haji, glancing inside the Field when he turned his attention to the Boulevard.

'We will become Companions,' stated Haji.

'I'm happy for you. And for her.'

'What about you and Cathy?' he asked. 'I assume you discussed about companionship with her when you were alone in the balcony?'

You remembered the moment when you and Cathy kissed. 'Sort of...but I decided not to be her companion.'

'For what reason?' Haji asked.

'For no reason,' you answered evasively, peering inside the Field again.

'If there is no reason, your decision does not make sense.'

'Well there is a reason,' you retorted with indifference. 'She kissed me when we were alone in the balcony. But I didn't feel anything. Anything other than her lips that is.'

Despite being surprised by knowing that Cathy had broken a Directive, he followed his line of reasoning, 'And you allowed the absence of feelings to serve as grounds for a decision?'

You shrugged and chuckled. 'I guess I did.'

'Why?' he asked, utterly confused.

You sighed. 'It just doesn't seem right to be with someone if you don't feel anything when you kiss her.'

'Alan, be reasonable,' and Haji's voice showed concern and care. 'You and Cathy have been friends since the start of apprenticeship and you haven't had anything but mutual agreement. As best as I can discern she seems to be the most suitable companion for you, and you are throwing away the opportunity to be with her out of lack of emotional response and risk Mother choosing someone with which you have no common interests at all.'

You stopped on your feet to ponder his point of view, while gazing at the clouded Panoramic Way. A feeling of anguish began to grow inside you and you felt more and more confused about your decision.

'You should not let feelings overcome reason Alan,' Haji said, concluding thoughts, and were his face not hiding under his facemask and you would have seen his witty smile.

You looked at him and smiled. 'You're probably right,' you admitted with modesty.

Then you approached the knee high wall and looked inside the Field, the gust of the Towers gently pulling you in. You glanced from side to side and when you made sure that no sentinel was watching, you raised one leg over the wall.

Almost immediately, you heard Haji's reprehensive whisper from behind you, 'Alan what are you doing?'

'What does it look like?' you answered. 'I'm stepping inside.'

'We are not allowed inside the Air Intake Fields. It is very dangerous. We could get caught by a draft and sucked into one of the air inlets.'

'All the more reason to see if there is a Specialist in need of assistance inside,' you retorted wittily.

'What?!' Haji's voice rose to a loud whisper, 'Do not climb that wall Alan Balthazar! Mother knows you will!'

Your feet landed on the pavement on the other side.

An eerie silence followed.

You looked back and smiled, 'Still haven't been contacted by Her.'

'Just wait and see. The sentinels will be here in no time,' he said, and his voice was now considerably aggravated for he was starting to realize you were beyond reasoning.

Still, the silence remained unbroken. No clanging of metallic feet was heard in the distance; only the quiet gust of air rushed above your heads.

You let out the thought that had been brewing in your mind, 'Haji I found the bracelet near the edge of this very Field. The Specialists could be hiding here. Don't you want to see the Torment for yourself?'

Haji looked at you quietly, his concern hiding behind the facemask. He was not unmoved by your appeal. Even so, he answered in sound judgement, 'Not if it implies being banned from Darm. Mother will know we are there! And the Torment is very dangerous. The Specialists are not themselves. We could be endangering our existences if they see us.'

'Well I am going,' you said stubbornly. 'And if I recall correctly you said you were accompanying me to see to my safety, did you not?'

'I did,' he said, knowing where that line of thought was headed.

You added in a mischievous manner, 'So, if I am going, you should come too, *adji*.'

He stared at you silently. Then he took a deep breath. 'This will not end well,' he said before stepping over the wall.

It was not long before you lost yourselves in the dark, quiet Field and neither Boulevard nor plasma barrier could be seen. Raging through you were furious gales of frozen air being sucked into the air inlets of the tall towers, whose beacons of light at their top faintly lit your way. The wind was relentless, and even though it was not strong enough to pull you into the air inlets, it was strong enough to hinder your movements significantly, and so you trudged on with great effort, towards where, you did not know.

'We will never find anything in this darkness,' you heard Haji's calm voice in your mind as the freezing gale raged through you.

The idea of being attacked without any warning by one of the manifestations presented to you in Fundaments of Existence was starting to make you feel nervous.

'A few more minutes and we leave,' you conveyed the thought him more to reassure yourself.

Suddenly, a shrill cry was carried by the wailing wind. Were it a scream you could not say, but its haunted echo had an ominous presence. You froze in place, peering into the darkness between the towers in front of you.

'Did you hear that?' you conveyed the thought to Haji.

'It seems to have come from there,' Haji's voice answered as he pointed into the dark labyrinth of towers to your left. Then his thought came with unease, *'Alan we should leave.'*

The sense that you were endangering your existences finally brought you to your senses. *'All right, you win. But let's leave through that way then,'* you answered, and stared heading towards the direction Haji had pointed.

No sooner had you felt your way around the first tower than something big hit you with such strength that your facemask flew off of your face and you were thrown to the metallic pavement. The connection you had established with Haji was immediately severed as an overwhelming dizziness engulfed your every thought.

Haji ran to you and kneeled. 'What happened?' he asked aloud, his voice greatly amplified by the facemask's speaker.

It felt like you had been struck in the head by a blunt object. Your head was spinning around so frantically that you had to shut your eyes and lay very still just to avoid losing consciousness. 'Something hit me,' you answered through clenched teeth.

Haji looked around nervously but saw nothing but darkness and heard nothing but the wind raging through his raised hood. To his surprise, three meters away from him, a body lying on the metallic pavement came into sight, steaming with water vapour. It wore a slim white exoderm, a lowered white hood and a black belt enveloped in crackling sparks on a slender waist.

'A Specialist,' Haji cried, even though he could not see more than a white figure.

When the figure would not stand up, he approached it cautiously.

'It's a girl,' he shouted through the gale between you. 'She seems unconscious.'

You risked opening your eyes a little bit to look at her, but without the facemask the freezing gale stung your eyes. 'Help me get up,' you shouted back.

Haji walked up to you, wrapped his arm around your back and helped you stand up as fast as you could manage. You head throbbed painfully, and the haziness you felt warned you that anything short of walking would send you back to the ground. Fighting the strong wind, you picked up your facemask, and after attaching it to your cold numb face you dragged your feet towards her and knelt next to Haji.

Haji pulled back the white exoderm on her left forearm. 'She is not wearing any Unit,' he said after examining her forearm. 'She has to be one of the missing Specialists.'

As you admired her soft angular chin beneath the lowered hood, you felt a sudden desire to pull her hood back.

Your eyes widened with bewilderment when you saw how beautiful her cool pale face was. Even more bewildering was her hair, white as unspoiled snow, and it shimmered as snow does when the soft rays of morning hours gleam upon its frozen surface.

...I know her face...

This was when you saw her for the first time, but the moment you laid eyes upon her you felt like you had known her for a long time. Time seemed to stop and the wind and towers faded into forgetfulness as you lost yourself admiring her beautiful face.

'If she is suffering from a manifestation, then it is the manifestation of beauty itself,' you said in an awe stricken tone.

'I am notifying Mother,' Haji shouted.

...stop him...

You shook your head, regaining your awareness.

'No!' you yelped. 'Wait!'

Breaking the link to his Unit, Haji stared at you and spoke apprehensively, 'Alan she might wake up at any moment. Then what will happen?'

As the dizziness slowly faded, your thoughts became clearer. 'Does she look like she's suffering from the Torment?' you insisted, and when you looked at her again you lost yourself admiring her beauty once more.

Haji looked at her and hesitated. His reply was lost in a disconcerting surge of hypotheses as to who she was, and after examining her attentively he began to suspect that she was not one of the Project Specialists, for she was not wearing any uniform or insignia and no Specialists was as young as she seemed to be. Her mere appearance seemed too otherworldly for a darmian even.

...help her...

'We have to help her,' you pleaded to him.

Even though Haji could not be entirely certain that she was not a Specialist, he felt that whoever she was, trying to help her would not end well for you and him.

'I don't think we should,' Haji shouted, the winds raging on relentlessly between you. 'I have a bad feeling about helping her.'

'Didn't you just tell me not to let feelings overcome reason?' you asked sternly.

Haji shook his head in disapproval.

'I'll carry her,' you promptly added. Ignoring the throbbing pain in your head, you lifted the girl to your arms. She was not very heavy, but she was tall for a girl, taller than you.

'And where do you propose we take her?'

'Out of this Field for a start,' you shouted back, and you glanced around before heading out.

Haji sighed and followed you.

...it almost seems as though my past self answered my calling when I urged him to help her...

In a manner of speaking he did, yet at the same time your desire to help her came to you as a reaction to what your past self felt, for your present and past self are part of the same consciousness. Given that consciousnesses are not bound to laws or dimensions, as we flow through the Tides of Fate, your present and past self become one and the same.

...then I can command myself to change the past...

You cannot. There is no way for any consciousness to tame the Tides of Fate be it by will or force. Even though you are one with your past self, you cannot *will* him to reshape the course of events, for causality does not apply to where you are. You are in a place that cannot be defined by time or space. The events you see here have already occurred in an infinite regression and at the same time are yet to occur in an infinite succession. You are merely a spectator, a ghost, bound by my will to the Tides of Fate.

...I do not understand...

It is not in your power to understand. It is beyond comprehension to any consciousness. But know this. All that is to come in your existence as Alan Balthazar has already come and pass. The Cosmos itself is but a fleeting shadow, an intangible light, and as you linger here in the ebb and flow of Life, you are seeing events as they truly are: visions and memories of eons long gone.

As you fled East through the countless towers your weariness began to grow and you started to lag behind Haji. Although the girl was not heavy, you – like all darmians - were not used to lifting weight, even less the weight of another, and your physical constitution was not developed far beyond the strength needed to carry the lightest of objects.

You leaned on a tower, your arms burning up from exhaustion. 'I cannot carry her any longer,' you shouted amidst your panting.

After gently laying the girl on the pavement you slid your back down the tower and sat on the floor.

Haji crouched beside you and waited in silence for you to recover.

As your strength slowly returned, your eyes were unconsciously drawn to girl once more. There was such calmness in her cool pale face that when you lost yourself admiring her something awakened deep inside you, a diffuse fervour that poured from within and overflowed to your skin like a filled lake breaking through a fragile dam.

'We have to hide her,' you said out of impulse.

'Have you lost all reasoning Alan?!' Haji burst out desperately. 'Stepping inside an Air Intake Field is a serious infringement, but what you propose is far from worse. She is most likely one of the missing Specialists and we are endangering our existences merely by being close to her! And Mother knows we are here,' he added gravely. 'Our best course of action is to leave her here and return to our residences.'

Haji would rarely lose his temper, and the fact that he did alerted you to the danger of what you were proposing. Still, you would not be discouraged. The sense of commitment towards the girl had become so strong that you would not think of anything other than helping her, 'If our Units have not yet received any notice from Her, chances are that She's not even aware of us being here.'

Strangely enough, as you spoke, the relentless winds were slowly abated, until an eerie quietness engulfed you.

Through the waning breeze, a faint clanging of metal came to your ears, distant at first, but every clang louder than the previous.

You and Haji stared at each other, halting your breath and standing completely motionless, hoping the sound would go away.

Clink. Clank. Clink. Clank. The sound was approaching rapidly now, becoming easily discernible. You realized it was coming from the darkness above. You and Haji lifted yourselves up and peered into the top of the towers. No air was being draw into them anymore. They had been deactivated.

Clank! Clank! Clank! Clank!

The last four *clanks* smashed the metallic pavement with the shape of four evenly spaced pairs of claws. Your heart started pounding in your chest when above the claw shaped marks, four slender droids, black as night, emerged out of thin air, encircling all three of you against the tower and denying you any chance to escape. You had never seen droids the likes of these before. They looked in many ways like sentinel droids but their structure was slimmer and lighter, their limbs more agile and slenderer, and they bore no insignia of the D.S.D. on their chests. They were Stalkers, droids designed for the sole purpose of capturing darmians who had strayed too far from Darm's purpose.

Through their featureless visages came the automated voice of Mother in unison, 'Apprentices Alan Balthazar and Haji Donovan, you are to relieve yourselves for peaceful arrest.'

Haji immediately dropped to his knees, bowing his head low and raising his arms forward so that his hands were out of his sight, following for the first time the Directive for arrest as best as he knew. Even though he was aware that there were severe consequences waiting ahead, he sighed with relief, believing that your senseless insurgency had been timely foiled, given that now you would have no other option but to obey Mother.

...what a fool...what short work he could have made of them if only he knew the power he held...

Contrary to what Haji had expected, you did not relieve or surrender, neither bowing your head nor raising your arms. You did kneel, however, to gaze down at the girl's beautiful face and lift her up by placing her right arm around your shoulder and your left hand around her waist. Then, you surrendered to the desire to rebel that screamed inside your head:

'No,' you said imposingly.

Haji looked at you and spoke in shock, 'Alan?! Obey Her command. I beg you!'

Despite your defiance, Mother did not falter. Each of the four stalkers raised one of their dark slender arms at you and from atop their forearms a small compartment with darts emerged. Her response was cold and uncaring:

'Apprentice Balthazar, you are to desist and surrender the specimen immediately. Failure to comply will lead to the use of tranquilizing darts.'

You felt the girl move and so you looked at her. She had lifted her head and opened her eyelids, revealing two deep blue eyes. They gleamed with a light of their own, dim at first, but becoming ever brighter.

With one effortless move one droid aimed his forearm at the girl's neck and fired a single dart; his aim was true and the dart carved itself in her bare neck. The girl grimaced, but at that moment, sparks erupted from the joints of the four droids and their heads and arms and legs began collapsing and they came falling to the ground simultaneously where they jerked in a spectacle of convulsions. When they stopped, the smell of burnt circuits emanated from their black inert shells.

'How?' said Haji, staring at the droids with incredulity.

The girl stared at you with her deep blue eyes. They were so compelling that you felt completely drawn to them. She opened her mouth as if to speak but moaned faintly, before her head collapsed onto your chest and the weight of her body surrendered hopelessly to the strength of your arms.

Worry overcoming you, you lowered her and gently laid her on the pavement. She was eerily still.

'This can't be good,' you said to yourself.

You hastily removed the strange object from her neck; its tip was filled with a single drop of her blood. You pulled the exoderm of your forearm back and allowed the drop to fall onto your Unit; then you issued it to scan the chemical components. The Unit conveyed to you that it had traces of *benzodiazepine*, a substance you knew to have sleep-inducing effects.

'She has been sedated,' you said, letting out a relived sigh and then looking at Haji, who was standing before the disabled droids fuming on the ground, his back turned to you.

'This incident is beyond reproach,' he said in complete dismay. 'It will most likely lead to our banishment. We will become Outcasts, like many before us.'

Upon hearing him, it struck you that he had just come from the Gathering, where he and Sophie had decided to become companions. He was a bright apprentice, one of the brightest of your generation, and all his expectations were close to being fulfilled. But now all seemed lost for him, and you were the sole responsible.

You shook your head in denial. 'The droids malfunctioned! We had nothing to do with that,' you blurted out.

Haji would not even turn to look at you. 'It doesn't matter. The little chance we had of leaving the field without alerting Mother is gone.'

You forced yourself to gather some sense but what had happened was too surprising. 'Haji this girl is not one of the missing Specialists. There is more to this than what we were made aware.'

'True as that may be, there is nothing we can do to help her,' he said dejectedly.

'Don't you want to know who she is?!'

Haji turned to look at you. 'Alan we will endanger our citizenship if we help her.'

The feeling that you had to help the girl was so strong that you promptly rejected his claim. You were determined to ensure her safety and you go as far as to ignore every Directive, confront any droid, forfeit your citizenship if you had to.

'There is nothing we can do Alan,' he said.

A reasonable solution came to your mind, 'We hide her in the Shelter. The dispersion field that envelops the chamber prevents any scans from detecting her. If we hide her there, she will be untraceable by any known sensors, even Mother's.'

Haji allowed himself to reason with you to try and make you understand the helplessness of the situation. 'Considering we manage to get there, how do you suggest we gain entry to the facility?'

'If we get there that won't be a problem,' you replied with confidence.

Your answer could only lead him to one conclusion. 'You know the emergency override code to the maintenance entrance?'

'I do. I saw it two weeks ago when Brent typed it in the touchscreen.'

'Mother changes those codes every day, Alan,' he stated.

'At least we have to try!'

Haji shook his head in dismay.

'Considering She has not changed it, how are we supposed to get there?' he asked condescendingly. 'We are to succeed in carrying the girl without alerting our presence to Mother?' he said, and following his line of thoughts his reasoning led him to the inevitable fact: 'Alan, we will be banished when we Mother finds us, or worse. We have no chance of success. Our best course of action is to leave the girl and present ourselves to Mother for peaceful arrest. There might still be a chance to avoid our banishment if we request an audience with the Council and receive their pardon,' he added in a warm consoling way.

...save her...that is all that matters...

You could not bear the thought of asking for the Council's pardon. For so many years you had followed their Directives against your will that you could not bear to subdue yourself to them, especially because you had done nothing wrong. Merged with that refusal, the desire to help the girl became so strong that you knew beyond doubt what you had to do. You clenched your fists and spoke in a grim voice, 'I will hide her in the Shelter. You should not come. This is my decision and I should face the consequences alone.'

You voice was so powerful that it imprinted itself on Haji's mind like an undeniable command. He was incapable of making you see reason and could only ask, 'You are willing to forfeit your citizenship for a girl you do not know?'

You gazed once more at the girl lying helplessly on the pavement. She seemed to be resting peacefully now.

'I will not let Mother have her,' you said with resolve.

Haji knew he could not reason with you any longer. He let out a frustrated sigh, glanced into the cold darkness that surrounded him and was drawn once more to the grave notion that he had broken several of the most important Directives that night.

'Then I will go with you,' he said.

Feeling suddenly overwhelmed with guilt, your voice lost all its command, 'Haji no! You should return to your residence.'

'I would never leave you alone *rabble-rouser*,' he said with warm compassion. 'Besides, my help will improve your odds of success.'

...I remember now...the day I incited my colleagues to skip indoctrinations...he has the same sense of purpose he had when he tried to stop the two Council Overseers from arresting me...

He was but a small young boy, yet he stood doggedly between you and the two tall figures of authority, denying them passage.

'But we cannot allow Mother to find out the location of the Shelter. That would doom Brent as well,' he added. 'Assuming that if we attempt to return to our residences we will be arrested, we are left with only one solution. We must activate the Signal Re-Router remotely.'

Activating the Signal Re-Router remotely meant giving up on everything Haji had planned for his future, and all that would be left for him would be the ominous void of uncertainty.

'Done,' he said and looked at you with lively eyes.

You were appalled with yourself for having forced him into helping you and you felt as weary and aged as one whose life is spent. You gave him a feeble smile from underneath your facemask and expanded your consciousness towards your Unit, focusing on conveying the thought of activating the Signal Re-Router.

'Done,' you said grimly. Then you lifted the girl to your arms. 'Let's go.'

...he risked his life to help me...

That is what a true friend does in times of need. But his actions were not entirely selfless. He found it deeply disturbing to see those menacing droids under Mother's command, and when he saw the girl wearing no Unit and seeming entirely unaffected by the Torment, he began to consider that the account of the missing Specialists had been a clever ruse forged to conceal what had really happened. It was an immensely disturbing thought for someone not accustomed to lies and deceit. He felt his trust in the Council was being put on trial and that learning the truth about the girl would be the defining action that would allow him to trust them once more. Therefore, he helped you not only because he was worried about your safety, but also because he needed to know the truth.

* * *

A droid leg was flattened beneath the weight of a metallic foot. Scattered between the deactivated Air Intake Towers were the four discomposed Stalkers. Wollen examined the surrounding area with his sensitive infrared sensors and found a faint trace of heat on the pavement. He approached it, minding his steps, and studied it. In the freezing temperatures the signature had all but disappeared and he could not make out what they meant.

He sniffed the stagnant air.

'The specimen. And an apprentice,' he reported, and his voice was vicious and distorted.

Watching him from the darkness was Mentalist Vittas, wearing his crimson robe, clad with gilded stripes on its shoulders. He had a proud look on his pale face and his gaze seemed to bear an omniscient awareness of everything that surrounded him. He looked down at Wollen, whose crouching form seemed like a misshapen amalgamation of flesh and metal.

'Two apprentices, whose curiosity and foolishness led them to the specimen. They are carrying her out of the field towards the Administrator Sector. Bring them to me as well,' he commanded in an impassive tone. 'Their actions cannot go unpunished.'

Wollen's maimed face lit with a rotten grin. 'With pleasure,' he answered in a ghoulish voice.

With unnatural ease, he leapt vertically, landing on the top of an Air Intake Tower twenty meters above, and then probed the darkened sea of towers with his cold monocle, attempting to find any heat signature.

'Wollen,' called the crimson Mentalist from below. 'You are not to harm them.'

Wollen's cheerful grin sunk underneath a frustrated sneer.

'Yes Master Vittas,' he answered before his form vanished into the night.

...hideous abomination...neither pyrean nor machine...

Not all cybernetic organisms are foul. To join life with machinery may seem unnatural, but they are still made of elements of the Cosmos, therefore they are still part of it. In the same sense there is no ingenuity of the living capable of overcoming My will, for all sentient creatures are bound to Me, therefore all that can be thought by them is still part of My will. Your ancestors found a name for this Law, even though they could not fully understand it. They named it the Plenitude Principle; others, somewhat less optimistically, named it Murphy's Law. That is why cybernetic organisms cannot be defined as acts of creation, but as acts of manipulation. As long as these Laws are held true, the boundaries of manipulation are practically endless.

...to seek immortality is to act against Your will...

That is true, for all who live must eventually face death. It is the cycle of Life and it is what binds all things together. You will come to learn throughout this journey that there are more unnatural things in the mind of the living than in the countenance of Wollen. However, Wollen was a particularly malignant creature, for he had been deprived of all kindness and compassion the moment he was transformed by Mentalist Vittas. His mind was filled with hatred for all unblemished life and the only appeasement he found was inflicting upon others the suffering that Vittas had inflicted upon him.

* * *

'I have to rest for a while,' you conveyed the thought to Haji.

You were breathing intensely through your facemask. Drops of sweat were rolling down its edges and dripping on the marbled pavement. Inside the relative safety of a dimly lit residential cloister, you laid the girl next to you and sat with your back against the outer wall of a residence. The night had become particularly cold and windy - a sign of the impending snowstorm - and when you removed your facemask to refresh yourself, the freezing air flooded your lungs and forced you to cough. You slapped your mouth and listened quietly, hoping that the coughing had not been detected by any sentinels marching on the streets just outside the cloister. To your relief, the only sound to be heard was of water trickling in the fountain at the centre of the cloister.

You removed your glove and touched the girl's face. Her skin was cold and hard. Worrying that the freezing temperatures would be too much for her to bear, you undressed your jacket and wrapped it around her face, tying a knot loose enough to allow her to breathe.

The polymerized edges of the facemask gently adhered to the shape of your face, restoring warm air to your lungs. You leaned your back on the wall and peered down the alley towards the street you intended to go. *'There are hardly any sentinels to be seen,'* you conveyed the thought to Haji. *'I would think that Mother would be more interested in finding us.'*

'There is definitely something wrong in all of this,' Haji answered back.

You gazed at the girl as she slept. 'Mother called her specimen. What do you think she meant by that? Could Specialist be experimenting on pyreans?' you spoke softly.

'I don't know,' Haji answered restlessly. 'But despite the shocking implications, that could very well be the case. The only explanation that I find as to why she is not manifesting is that they have succeeded in finding a cure for the Torment and tried to apply it to themselves. Perhaps that is why they removed their Units.'

'Perhaps,' you said absentmindedly; you were thinking about the moment the droids malfunctioned. She was staring at them with a glow in her eyes, a deep blue glow.

Haji muttered, 'But we don't have time to consider the reasons. We must leave. Haste is essential if we are to succeed.'

His words pulled you back to the present. You peered once more into the street and made sure there was no sentinel patrolling it. Re-establishing the link to his Unit, you conveyed the thought to him, *'Let's go. Your turn to carry her and my turn to see if the way is clear.'*

'I am regretting my decision in helping you already,' he answered as he lifted the girl into his arms.

Haji followed you close behind as you crossed the street towards the next residential cloister, only to cross the cloister onto the next street. You repeated this process with growing effectiveness, always looking around the corners of the alleys before stepping out, always attentive to the sounds coming from the streets, always hoping that neither clink nor clank would resound off the rooftops. After many cloisters had been left behind and many casual patrols of sentinels avoided, the time to enter the Manufacturing Sector drew upon you.

Standing at the end of one of the last alleys before the bright East Boulevard, you and Haji studied the two pairs of sentinels that guarded it, performing their mechanical back and forth march. They swept a segment of fifty meters, each pair patrolling a separate lane of the Boulevard, and they moved in opposite directions so that their combined line of sight granted them a seemingly flawless perception of the Boulevard. Fortunately, you were aware that sentinel visual sensors had a field of vision limited to *135°*, a specification that not many darmians were aware of, but something that had helped you and Haji avoid them on many occasions on your journeys to the Shelter.

Studying their perfectly synchronized march, Haji noticed that if you crossed the lanes just as both pairs turned their backs to each other you could reach the other side before they turned around at the end of their segment. To accomplish this, the timing and speed had to be flawless; but you had mastered an activity that was much alike the task. To you, it was as simple as calculating a drifter jump between the paths of two other drifters.

Waiting for the right moment, you conveyed to Haji a concern that was starting to trouble you, *'When Brent finds her in the Shelter we will be in a lot of trouble.'*

'Let's worry about getting her inside the Shelter first,' Haji answered. *'Go, now!'*

You left the alley, sprinting across the dry pavement, the warm gust of wind coming from the ventilation boxes muffling the sound of your footsteps as the sentinels marched away from you. When you reached the alley at the other end, you turned to see Haji lagging behind as the sentinels finished their segments, and for a moment you felt that he was going to be detected.

Haji crossed the Boulevard just before the sentinels turned around, stopping by your side as the clinking of footsteps passed by.

He sighed with relief. *'Flawless,'* he conveyed while panting from carrying the girl.

'Just like beating Zigvirat,' you returned the thought while chuckling.

Haji allowed himself to chuckle with you as he recovered his breath.

In that moment of respite you looked back to the alley where you had been before and you thought you saw the odd gleam of a metallic figure. Its shape was too bent and distorted by the mist released from a ventilation box to make out, but it did not seem a droid for its head did not have the same metallic gleam like his chest. You were trying to make out what it was when Haji nudged you.

'Come. We're still not out of danger.'

You nodded to him.

With haste and caution, you covered the distance to the Shelter through the alleys and streets of the tall facilities. For the first time in your existence you had lingered in the streets well into Sleep Time, and the same course you were so used to take on peaceful bright afternoons, now carried with it an ominous darkness and a strange silence that warned you to be doubly aware. It had not been the first time you had broken a Directive, nor would it be the last, but never to this point. Mother was actively searching for you, and it was only a matter of time until She found and arrested you. Yet for all your worry, there was still not a single sentinel to be seen. The Manufacturing Sector was no more than a dark abandoned place, whose dark empty streets and tall shadowy buildings resembled more the surreal constructs of nightmares than the prominent Manufacturing Facilities of Darm. Even worse, was the heavy snow that started to pour down on you, a sign that the snowstorm had arrived.

You halted at a snowy alley, three alleys away from Brent's, and waited for Haji as he stopped next to you, struggling to hold the girl on his arms.

'*Let's carry her together,*' you conveyed. '*There doesn't seem to be any sentinel here.*'

As you lifted the girl's arm over your shoulder, a slow repetitive clinking crept down the narrow walls. You immediately looked up at the facility's rooftops, but saw only falling snow. The thought of black droids suddenly emerging out of thin air and surrounding in you in that narrow alley rooted you in place. You glanced at both ends of the alley, staring for what seemed an eternity.

'Run,' you whispered feebly.

A hideous laughter echoed down the walls. This time, when you looked up, there was something looming over the edge of one facility, something bearing a strange resemblance to a pyrean crouching in an odd fashion and staring down at you, his head bowing low, his hands gripping the edge of the roof between his feet, its bent knees pointing upwards. His face was too darkened to make out, yet its misshapen form seemed unlike anything you had ever seen.

Startled by that apparition you stared to run down the alley, sharing the burden with Haji as you both carried the girl on your shoulders, but just as you were reaching the street, you and Haji recoiled as a plume of snow lifted into the air before you when something heavy smashed the pavement. As the plume settled, you saw to your shock he who was staring at you from the roof now standing before you as clearly and vividly as needed be. His appearance was grotesque, a tall long-limbed body made of decayed flesh and silvery metal, all bound together by screws and sutures. His muscular legs were a concoction of flesh and pneumatics with sturdy metal kneecaps and metallic feet; his bare abdominals were surmounted by a wide chest clad in silvery armour; his bare left arm was overly muscular, layered in decomposed flesh, while his right arm was made of metal and pneumatics with a metallic claw as a hand.

Wollen cast a terrifying gaze at you with his dark monocle and a pale gray eye surmounted by a scarred forehead. 'Going somewhere?' he asked in a harsh synthesized voice.

You stared at that strange spectacle of misshapen flesh and bolted metal, all the while thinking that in no way could the crude contraption in front of you be one of the missing Specialists.

'What are you?' you asked with incredulity.

Wollen let out a sinister chuckle and extended his claw-like metallic hand. 'Hand her over,' he ordered, exposing a gruesome line of rotten teeth as he grinned.

You were too perplexed to reply, but not perplexed enough to forget the task at hand. Empowered by the sense of commitment towards the girl, you placed her on Haji's arms and conveyed the thought to him, *'Take her to the Shelter. The code is "S-U nine-two-four".'*

Then you stepped forth, challenging the frightening pyrean.

Haji would not argue with you; the sight of that mixture of flesh and machine had baffled him beyond words. He nodded and headed back to the way he came, dragging the girl beside him.

Wollen feigned a left hook to your face. When you ducked, he leapt over you like an agile animal and thrust himself towards Haji. Sensing his approach, Haji threw himself onto the snowy pavement just before he was struck in the back, the girl falling next to him.

Unimpressed by his quick reaction, Wollen halted his momentum and bent over him, extending his hand as if to help him stand up. 'I will not let you run, so why not spare yourself from a beating and come with me, nicely?' he asked with unfitting formality, almost like that of a citizen of Darm.

Fuelled by a desperate rush of adrenaline, you recalled all the fighting that took place in the halls of the Drifter Races and dashed towards him, lunging at him, feet first, and clashing against his silvery back; he rolled down the deep alley until the blanket of snow halted him.

'Go, now!' you said aloud.

Haji heard you plainly. He jumped to his feet, lifted the girl to his arms and ran past you. As you saw him leave, he disappeared into the snowy darkness. It was up to you to stop Wollen from chasing him.

'You should not have done that,' you heard him speak sombrely.

You turned to look at him, three meters away from you, only to see him rise to his feet and calmly wipe the snow from his shoulders. Ignoring the urge to flee, you gazed around, searching for something that would help you confront him, but there were no objects in the dark alleys of the Manufacturing Sector. You stepped backwards nervously, clenching your fists, crushing the dread that ran rampant through your body, 'Come any closer and I'll do it again,' you provoked, the voice projected from your facemask trembling with doubt.

Wollen chuckled scornfully and twisted its neck from side to side to extend its muscles, his joints snapping softly. 'I might just have to, but I doubt you will even see me,' he said just before he encroached upon your listless body with impossible speed and struck you with an overpowering blow the stomach.

You immediately fell to your knees, coughing uncontrollably.

Staring down at your defeated posture, he said with displeasure, 'Are you ready to give up? Or do I need to beat you up a little more?'

Ignoring the nauseating pain, you jumped to your feet and aimed a succession of angered jabs to his head, but none made contact as Wollen leaned back with ease. Your strength slowly draining away with each consecutive miss, you aimed one desperate fist at his bare abdomen. Wollen did not dodge it. He did not have to. His solid abdomen took the blow without so much as budging while the impact almost broke your wrist. Looking down at your quavering body, he chuckled in his deformed timbre and with one single swooping kick to the abdomen he sent you tumbling down the alley.

After you came to a stop, you crossed your arms around your abdomen. Wollen allowed you to recover, staring at you in an unimpressed manner as you sat on your knees, moaning and struggling to breathe. It was hard for you to accept, but you had no chance of stopping the heinous pyrean standing in front of you. You were hopelessly outmatched and the only thing that prevented you from succumbing to the debilitating chest pain was the unmitigable desire to help the girl. And as you clung to that thought, her deep blue eyes came into your mind, her soft cool face grimacing as her head collapsed against your chest. Even if you could not stop him, to the least you would ignore the pain a little longer and use your remaining strength to stall him for as long as you could.

...*confidence comforts*...

A sense of calmness enveloped you as an unusual sense of confidence overcame your thoughts. You removed your facemask, exposing your face to the freezing air and gazed peacefully at the pyrean's maimed countenance five meters away from you. He did not seem unsightly anymore, nor did he seem menacing. He was merely someone, something, a thing that had to be stopped.

...*courage fortifies*...

Wollen growled and charged towards you, building up a relentless momentum. His attack would most certainly injure you severely, but you did not falter. You stood your ground, focusing on the single purpose of stopping it. He aimed his knee at your chest, but you did not lose heart. You crossed your forearms before you, driven by the desire to withstand it, even if it would ultimately cost you your very existence.

...resolve protects...

Suddenly, your eyes were kindled with the red glow of resolve as all your consciousness was engulfed by that overwhelming emotion. Your forearms were flooded by a burning torrent of blood and the exoderm was torn asunder by a myriad of red crystals that erupted from your skin. Wollen's knee smashed against it furiously, but the crystal shell held firm, receiving the blow without shattering and projecting a bright flash that for a second tinted the dark alley in crimson.

The blow knocked you and Wollen to the ground, and after you scrambled to your feet, you could only but stare in awe, your eyes widened upon the thick shell of red crystals softly gleaming on your forearms. You could not comprehend that inexplicable metamorphosis, but before you could make any sense of it, Wollen - who had already gotten up - aimed a foot at your chin; out of reflex, you blocked the attack with one forearm, and once more the red crystals deflected the blow, projecting a bright crimson flash and casting Wollen back.

Excitement overflowed through you as you realized you now had something you could defend yourself with, and without any other thought you aimed your fist at Wollen's awe stricken face. This time Wollen did not lean back, to your own misfortune; for when your fist struck the creature's face you felt a sting of pain so intense that before you knew it you were down in the ground, grabbing your wrist with a cry stuck in your throat. When you peered at it there were no more crystals on your skin; your frail bones had been too weak to withstand the impact and your wrist had shattered. The pain was excruciating, and even before you could overcome it, Wollen grabbed the collar of your exoderm and lifted you into the air; then he thrust you against the wall, grabbing your left forearm and staring at its back. When he saw your Unit properly adhered to the skin he was baffled. He leaned towards you in until his face stopped a breath away from yours.

'How were you able to manifest?' he asked in a commanding tone, his breath reeking of rotten teeth.

When you would not stop moaning in pain, he threw you towards the other wall. Your back and head smashed against it; your sight was filled by an explosion of sparkling lights, and unrelenting waves of wooziness sapped all the remaining strength from you. You collapsed over the snowy pavement, and as you teetered on the edge of consciousness, you heard an irritated growl and a statement filled with disdain, 'Pitiful.'

...if only I could harness them...

'Alan!' Haji screamed, as he ran towards your fallen body.

He kneeled right in front of the Wollen, ignoring him altogether, and turned you upwards. You head drooped down but your lips still moved. He leaned one ear close to your mouth and heard you moaning faintly. There was still some consciousness left in you. He saw your facemask fallen on the snow, the falling snowflakes piling upon it, picked it up and attached it to your face. Then looked up at the creature, which seemed to be immersed in calm contemplation, and spoke angrily, 'You mindless thing! Why would you harm him?'

His awareness suddenly aroused, Wollen looked down at him and saw that the girl was no longer with him.

'Where is the girl?' he promptly asked with a clear commanding voice.

His voice was so powerful that Haji was utterly compelled to answer; however, instead of revealing her location he forced himself to answer evasively, 'I do not know which girl you are talking about.'

Wollen approached his maimed face and asked menacingly, 'Where is the girl you found in the air intake field?'

Haji tried clenched his teeth and tried to resist the commanding voice. 'She is beyond your reach,' he answered evasively.

'Where is she,' Wollen asked again, and his voice was becoming impatient. 'Tell me now.'

It took Haji a painful amount of self-control to remain quiet. Ignoring the command and the pain triggered by his defiance, he focused on trying to find the best way to rescue both of you from that precarious situation. He soon determined the best option and quickly put it in practice, expanding his mind to his Unit to alert Mother to his presence. However, a lingering thread of reasoning warned him that the creature would stop him with a vile attack.

It was precisely what Wollen did. Noticing his blank stare and realizing just what he was trying to do, Wollen swung his fist at his face with a clean right hook that would have knocked him out cold and put a swift end to his attempt; however, Haji instinctively ducked and the clenched claw grazed his green hood, throwing it back.

Wollen stared at him for a moment, surprised by his timely reaction; he had swung his fist so fast that Haji could not have seen it coming, yet he had managed to avoid it.

...to every action there is a reaction...

It is what came to be known as causality. And Haji's understanding of causality, combined with his will, allowed him to foresee the event just before it occurred. And for the minutes that followed, he continuously foresaw every jab, hook and uppercut Wollen threw at him, avoiding them altogether, either dodging, ducking or rolling over the snowy pavement. Angered with his ability to dodge him, Wollen went on a relentless rampage and the confrontation prolonged for many unwavering minutes of concentration without presenting any victor; however, even if Haji succeeded in avoiding every strike, he had not a second to reason what was happening. To him, he felt as if he was deeply immersed in a trance that granted him sight of the Wollen's movements just before he actually moved. The premonitions became so familiar that he was beginning to gain the upper hand, and with the advantage, he was allowed to plan a cunning counter-assault. Ducking a hook, he kicked a tuft of loose snow from the pavement, blanketing the air between them; exploiting the dim visibility he executed a flying double kick, mimicking with perfect accuracy the movement he saw you perform moments before. A brute force travelled from his snow-screened feet to his legs and he knew he had struck the creature. He fell from the impact, the mantle of snow cushioning his fall, and hastily expanded his consciousness to his Unit, utterly breaking his awareness. From the blanket of snow, on came a jab that hit his chest knocking the air out of his lungs hurtling him to the ground.

The snow settled only to reveal Wollen's contemptuous grin. 'You only blind yourself.'

Dumbfounded, Haji tried to understand just how the creature saw his move. It could not be an infra-red sensor for the cold snow would blind all heat emission all the same.

Understanding Haji's incredulous stare, the creature tapped with one finger on the metallic plate that coated most of its skull next to what seemed to be an ear cavity.

'Ever heard of pressure waves?' he asked.

No sooner had he spoken than Haji realized he was no match for the creature. When he came to terms with the dire situation he was in, he knew his only solution was to run to the street and alert any sentinels passing by. But he recovered his concentration only to foresee another onslaught of jabs, hooks and kicks. After countless near hits, when he had finally managed to gain some ground and near one end of the alley, the creature dashed past him with impossible speed. With his back turned against him, Haji sensed that some new unknown threat was imminent and he immediately threw himself to the ground, just before a lance sprouted from Wollen's hand and struck the impermium wall, resounding like a sharp hammer striking a solid metal block.

Haji rolled over one shoulder and quickly got up. It was then he saw the long lance sprouting from the creature's metallic arm pricking the left wall. The lance slowly recoiled inside his claw as Wollen stood upright, staring at him calmly.

'Impressive,' he said. 'But I doubt you will be able to avoid this.'

Wollen's face was filled with an expression of sheer anger and his pale gray eye blazed with a bloody red gleam; suddenly, the fleshy arm grew to twice its size, his clenched hand becoming like a solid block of flesh.

The shock of what Haji was seeing broke his awareness and what could have been a prediction of a vicious blow suddenly became the blow itself. The creature's bulging hand flew against his chest giving him only the time to raise his forearms to block it. The impact was so overwhelming that it shattered one of Haji's forearms and propelled him backwards, making him lose his balance and grimace from the sharp pain. Still managing to stand on his feet, Haji was quickly overwhelmed by another vicious barrage of jabs that lit the alley in crimson each time Wollen's hand struck him, before one hook to the face sent Haji's facemask flying to one side and his body crashing to the ground.

The freezing wind pierced his face and he grimaced, his eyelids shut, his teeth clenched. His body was aching, feeling the metallic flavour of his own blood wandering around his mouth as he rolled on the floor. He heard the creature's footsteps crunching the snow as he approached.

Wollen dropped to one knee and drew his scarred face close to Haji's kind face, now flushed from the cold, and with the facemask lying on the tip of his thin metallic fingers he brought the facemask to Haji's face and squeezed it abruptly and unkindly.

Now that his face was inside the protective layer Haji sat on his legs and opened his eyes to see the abominable creature merely a breath away; he saw his raging expression return to a calm deformed countenance and his arm collapse back to its normal, albeit still muscular size.

'Now. Are you ready to tell me where you hid the specimen?' Wollen asked with his harsh voice, its warm breath fogging up Haji's facemask visor.

A thought warned Haji how easy it would be to carve a swift right hook on the creature's soft fleshy left cheek and just after he foresaw the success he jammed it on his face. The punch did not carry much strength, for he was close to exhaustion, but the force was sufficient enough for his fist to rip though the creature's decomposed flesh and sink into its teeth, the jaw detaching itself and his head coiling to the side.

Haji rose quickly to his feet and gained some distance.

'Not quite ready yet.'

Wollen shook his head, disapproving of Haji's foolishness. He reattached his jaw and spat a pair of rotten teeth into the white snow, smearing it with spatters of dark blood.

Just as Haji stared attentively at the creature, trying to foresee its next assault, a thought erupted in his mind that he would soon be hurtling to the ground. Before he could understand the thought, his mind suddenly became shrouded in darkness.

The last thing he saw was the blood red ember gleaming on the Wollen's pale gray eye just before he vanished. He felt a crushing blow to his face, his feet lifted off the ground as his body spun in mid air, and he fell face down to the snow. His lungs drew one last meagre breath before his heart gave out.

...not even after a thousand deaths would I spare you from retribution...

'You shouldn't have done that,' you muttered.

Standing next to Haji's lifeless body, Wollen turned to look at you. He crossed his arms patiently and chuckled at your feeble attempt to drag yourself along the wall towards him. He leaned his head onto the left shoulder and sneered in contempt.

'Haven't you had enough?' he asked.

With two simple hops he covered the distance between you and sunk a knee in your ribs. The air from your lungs was sucked out and a crushing pain rendered you breathless. When you fell on the ground gasping for air that refused to enter your lungs, he gripped your head with his enormous fleshy hand and lifted you from the ground. You felt your skull being crushed by the tremendous pressure and out of sheer instinct for survival your unharmed hand to grab his wrist, crying in pain.

He chuckled mockingly when he saw tears rolling down your anguished face. 'Tell me where your friend took the girl and I will stop.'

The piercing cold worsened your efforts to breathe. You could barely open your eyes, but still you opened them and locked them onto the creature's pale eye. Your innocent young features shifted from gentleness to sombreness as if your had become a grim, proud pyrean and you uttered in a coarse voice, 'You will never find her.'

Wollen widened a rotten smile.

'My, my...she is fast to work her charm,' he mocked. 'My Master told me she is the most beautiful thing one can lay eyes upon. That a mere glance from her can steal one's will. I might just have my fun with her before I deliver her to him,' he said and licked his chapped lips with a horrendous dark tongue.

Your eyes were kindled with rage as you growled through gritted teeth.

Upon seeing your anger, Wollen was struck with wonder and delight. 'You want to stop me? You want to hurt me for what I did to your friend?'

He clenched his claw around your left forearm and you felt a surge of electricity course through your body, causing you to writhe in uncontrollable spasms. Sharp pain stung your mind as your Unit died away.

'Show me how much,' he said, his deformed voice burning through the sharp pain, consuming your every thought.

A fiery rage took complete hold of you. All the pain was suppressed by a burning sensation and your body began growing in size, your head becoming too large for Wollen's hand to grasp. With one increasingly growing hand your grabbed his stretched out arm and with uncontrollable strength snapped it in two with a single crushing grip. Then you clenched your other hand around his neck and lifted him high above the ground, his feet flapping away as you choked him. You had become almost twice his size and your face had been twisted beyond recognition, becoming the face of wrath, eyes burning like two boiling embers, gritted teeth crushing the uncontrollable rage.

...I will destroy you...

When you spoke those words your voice was unlike any other uttered sound. It was guttural, seeming more the deep bellow of a beast than the voice of a young pyrean. Your oversized hand was about to snap Wollen's neck when something cold pierced into your abdomen, drove through your gut and erupted from your back. You looked down to see a long silver lance plunged into your abdomen. Without any warning the cold lance was instantly heated, singing your insides and cauterizing the wound. You were sapped by a shock wave of pain and were immediately deprived of all the rage that flowed through your body. Your overgrown hand, once firmly clenched around the Wollen's neck, collapsed back to its normal size and fell limp at your side; and as your body slowly shrunk to its normal size, you sunk to your knees and keeled over, face down in the snow.

* * *

A chilling wind blew on your face as your consciousness sunk into an ever darker abyss. In its last flicker, you felt a remote and repetitive clanking of metal striking metal. You heard the waning murmur of a heart. You sensed it skip a beat, and then pulsate hesitantly. It thumped once more, faintly, and then again, strong and lively, as one announcing the deathly silence that follows...

Prelude to Ascension

A single resounding boom echoed in a darkened void. In the still silence that followed, the boom slowly rose to a persistent thumping, whose vibrant waves began to stir the darkness. Beleaguered by the unrelenting clamour, an entity began its sluggish awakening, slowly becoming aware of the resonance that threatened to destroy the dark foundations where it had slept for an eternity. The walls of the void began to crack, and from the gaps that began to form sprouted slender beams of light that bathed the entity with an indistinct sense of warmth. The pitch-black shards started to fall into the infinite void like the last drops of rain of an everlasting night, and the entity slowly realized that the break of a new dawn had begun. Drop by drop they fell, as the unremitting clamour shattered the lingering foundations, until it felled the very last shard with the last clamour, which was clearer, stronger, more vibrant than any other, culminating in a blast of light that vanquished the darkness and engulfed the entity. And where once was dark, now there was light. And it was then that the entity became aware of herself. Her senses awoke, and she felt the warm embrace of the light surrounding her, and heard for the first time the distant singing that echoed throughout an intangible golden mist. Like voices from a choir bound together by harmony they sang, and she felt the desire to merge herself with them, and so she did. And she felt their presence surround her, become her. She rejoiced, for now she knew her eternal solitude had come to an end. Now she was a whole, a golden mist formed by a boundless host of souls that sang to her an eternal gestalt of music.

End of Part I of Ascension

Dear reader,

It is my greatest wish that you enjoyed reading Visions of Gaea. If you would like to support Visions of Gaea please leave a rated review at the book's page in www.amazon.com. It is a small gesture, but it is of great help.

If you wish to become part of Visions of Gaea project or leave any suggestions for the upcoming visions, feel free to contact me at ruifrvaz@gmail.com.

May your will help you accomplish your dreams,
R. R. Vaz

Glossary

[1] A holoprojector is one of the two server interfaces used in Darm. Physically, it resembles a spherical shaped structure hovering over a bowl-shaped base. It is mainly composed of laser reflectors capable of projecting a three-dimensional image anywhere around it.

[2] A neuropad is one of the three Neural Devices used in Darm. Physically, it is a malleable sheet mainly composed by synthetic neurons attuned to the frequency of a darmian's Personal Identification Unit. It is capable of recording any information - be it auditory, olfactory or visual - via Thought Interaction.

[3] The Standings is a real-time ranking of apprentices. Mother continually assigns each apprentice to a standing according to their highest earned credits. At the end of apprenticeship, the top one-hundred finalists are awarded with the Highest Distinction.

[4] Cognitive Rehabilitation is a neurologic procedure that rearranges neural pathways to remove unwanted beliefs and enhance desired ones, consequently altering behaviour patterns and personality traits.

[5] Sentinels are droids from the Darmian Security Division. They are Mother's physical presence in Darm and they allow Mother to ensure that darmians uphold the Directives established by the Council.

[6] Permaglass is a virtually indestructible glass primarily composed of aerogel and graphene sheets. Once it was commercialized, regular glass became obsolete due to its friability and low thermal insulation.

[7] A server is a standard quantum computer equipped with synthetic neurons which allow for Thought Interaction with a User's Personal Identification Unit.

[8] A ventilation box is one of the components of the Environment Generator, which is an atmospheric control system that regulates the air inside the metropolis. The EG extracts the cold oxygen-depleted air from the atmosphere and expels warm oxygen-enriched air.

[9] Fibreconcrete is regular concrete reinforced with 5% of graphene fibres. Graphene dramatically increases the tensional resistance of the concrete, rendering it impervious to cracking and rupture caused by traction and compressing forces as well as projectile impact.

[10] Electrodynamic induction is the wireless transmission of electricity between two or more coils that are highly resonant at the same frequency.

[11] A holoscreen is one of the two server interfaces used in Darm. Physically, it is a thin malleable sheet capable of emitting holographic images, providing the user with a realistic sense of depth.

[12] A neuroglove is one of the three Neural Devices used in Darm. It communicates with a server through specific hand gestures, where each delicate finger and hand movement corresponds to a predefined thought.

[13] The psysis is a gastian device that directly connects a user to a server. By emitting electric impulses to the brain, it is capable of inducing a user into a lucid dream and enabling him to enter a customizable dream world.

[14] Field of View - or FoV - became a commonly used term in the dream world. Its popularity grew amongst players with the development of the Real Action Shooter "*Swoosh!*" which allowed a very wide FoV, the widest being 270°.

[15] Although combustion engines were rendered obsolete after the discovery of Gravity Propulsion, the excitement that every gastian shared for the incandescent jets of plasma and the collisions ending in spectacular explosions safeguarded its place in many games.

[16] Heads-up Display is a term vastly employed in the dream world. Its origin has long confounded historians. However, some believe it was employed by the antigans to describe a form of interface used on their technological constructs.

[17] A ring-slap is a technique that consists in slapping the ring-rudders of an opponent's drifter to attempt to damage them. By destroying both ring-rudders the drifter loses steering capability and eliminating the racer becomes as easy as *"lifting a ton with an anti-grav gun."*

[18] Pinching is a type of Elimination that consists in destroying a drifter by smashing it between two other drifters.

[19] Also known as *ARMTraP,* as players came to refer to it after an incident where Messir - a forcibly retired player - had his avatar's arm disintegrated when attempting to prevent his opponent from escaping a brawl that erupted in his pit.

[20] All information in Darm is stored in Mother's internal Database. Although She possessed all the knowledge of the Nova Pyre, access was granted based on levels of clearance to prevent sensitive information from becoming accessible to the general population.

[21] One of the five buildings of the Hub and the place where all data and artifacts recovered from the Age of Antiga Pyre and the subsequent Age of Obscurity are in display.

[22] Impermium is a metal alloy composed of 33% of *graphene* fibres, which render it impervious to erosion or stain. Due to the extraordinary resilience of *graphene* (200 times stronger than steel) any higher concentration would result in a needless excess.

[23] A neurolink is one of the three Neural Devices used in Darm. It is the only neurodevice exclusive to the citizens, and it allows its wielder Thought Interaction with Mother and direct access to Her extensive Database.

[24] Food generators are Darm's "cooks". They are connected though a sterilized piping system to the food manufacturing facilities and serve a personalized Recommended Daily Dosage of nutrients on each plate.

[25] A residence is granted to every apprentice upon achieving citizenship. Each residence is occupied in pairs and all finalists are granted the opportunity to choose

a companion from the opposite gender. Each pair was appointed with one and only one descendant at a time.

[26] An appliances room contains every devices required to maintain a residence habitable. Examples of devices are the food generator, cutlery dispenser, multipurpose washer and an oval-shaped cleaning drone whose task is to keep the residence clean.

[27] A nanosheet is a memory device capable of storing digital information from a neuropad. Although eidetic and sensory memory storage assumed a predominant role in Darm's neuro technologies, their effectiveness kept them as the primary device for information storage.

[28] An exoderm is a bio-synthetic membrane that adheres to skin tissue. It is flexible and removable and remains alive due to a symbiotic process with the wearer by effecting gaseous and liquid trades and recycling waste products of the body.

[29] Magtubes are conduits that utilize magnetic fields to carry any passenger inside them to different levels of a building. The fields interact with superconducting slits inside any footwear and gloves. Speed and direction are controlled using Though Interaction with the magtube servers.

[30] When a restrictive collar is attached to the neck it confines the area of freedom of its wearer to the interior of an abstract sphere centred on a restrictive marker. If the wearer trespasses the confined area, the collar automatically renders him unconscious.

[31] Helium is the primary coolant used in Darm. Although Helium is a rare gas in Artica, fusion of Hydrogen atoms allowed for the production of synthetic Helium, which is equal to regular Helium.

[32] The Radiation Dispersion Device engulfs matter inside an energy field that redirects outside radiation around it so that the matter inside remains invisible. As to the radiation emanating from the inside the field disperses it through the ground, leaving a characteristic heat trail behind.

[33] Eternium is a high temperature superconductor. Through electric induction *eternium* is able to generate a magnetic field strong enough to repel or attract objects by exerting forces of several orders of magnitude.

[34] A plasma barrier is composed of a super-condensed plasma confined to an internal electromagnetic field. The plasma prevents the permeability of any matter while the electromagnetic field prevents the plasma from leaking.

[35] According to a popular anecdote, some pyreans believe that the name *odyr* actually derived from the expression *"Oh dear!"* which was the screaming interjection of the first pyreans that saw these creatures.

[36] Weeks in Darm had six days: five Work Days and one Rest Day.

[37] In Darm, gold is as abundant and inexpensive as any other chemical element and can be easily aquired with credits. Upon request, Darm's facilities manufacture Council-sanctioned objects out of any combination of chemical elements, regardless of complexity and shape.

Made in the USA
Columbia, SC
11 January 2020